BOUNDLESS
AS THE SKY

FABLES & TALES,

SOME OF THEM TRUE

DAWN
RAFFEL

Sagging
Meniscus

Some of these pieces initially appeared in the following journals, sometimes in slightly different form: *BOMB*, *New World Writing*, *The Northwest Review*, *Big Other*, *Exacting Clam*, *Firmament*, *Tammy: A Journal*, *Foreign Lit*, *No Tokens*, *Exquisite Pandemic*, *Mom Egg*, *People Holding*, *Five Points*, *Logue*, *New Flash Fiction Review* , and in the Ravenna Press *Artefakta* series. In addition, some stories appeared in the following anthologies: *Providence Noir*, edited by Ann Hood (Akashic), *XO Orpheus*, edited by Kate Bernheimer (Penguin), *Best Small Fictions 2015*, selected by Robert Olen Butler (Queens Ferry Press), *Best Small Fictions 2016*, selected by Stuart Dybek (Queens Ferry Press), *Best Microfictions 2021*, selected by Amber Sparks (Pelekinesis Press) and *Best Small Fictions 2021* selected by Nathan Leslie and Rion Amilcar Scott (Sonder Press).

Set in Mrs Eaves XL with LᴬTEX.

ISBN: 978-1-952386-41-1 (paperback)
ISBN: 978-1-952386-42-8 (ebook)
Library of Congress Control Number: 2022941821

Sagging Meniscus Press
Montclair, New Jersey
saggingmeniscus.com

For Mike, Brendan, and Sean

Contents

Part Two: Boundless as the Sky

Illustrations

The Lost City: photographed by the author using black-and-white Fuji film and a Nikon camera, circa 1980. Most of the original collection was lost in a flood.

Death mask of François de Charette: Selbymay, CC BY-SA 3.0, via Wikimedia Commons.

Sally Rand: performing the infamous dance for which she was repeatedly arrested.

Crowd waiting to welcome Italo Balbo in Chicago: ©Arnoldo Mondadori Editore S.p./agefotostock.

Balbo smoking: photographed in Chicago, July 16, 1933, cropped by the author. Standing next to Balbo were Father Aristo Simoni and an unidentified woman.

BOUNDLESS AS THE SKY

The Author

She covered her face.

She tore the damp stuffing out of the past and filled her fists with synonyms. Flung words like confetti, like fairytale feathers, repeating herself again and again.

She believed, in this way, she could bring back the dead, if just this once.

PART ONE

THE CITY TOWARD WHICH MY JOURNEY TENDS

If I tell you that the city toward which my journey tends is discontinuous in space and time, now scattered, now more condensed, you must not believe the search for it can stop.

—Italo Calvino, *Invisible Cities*

The Beautiful City of Serena

In the beautiful city of Serena, every old woman wears a mask. The body may yet appear lithe in slacks, in silks, in exquisitely calculated jackets; the gait still steady in the cleverest shoes. The hair is calibrated to perfection, dyed, snipped. And yet the face—the face!—cannot be made to please the eye, not by needle, by knife, nor emollient, unguent, pressure, laser, poison, paint. And so the old women go about in vivid masks: the poor in the primary colors; the wealthy in the jewel tones, garnet and sapphire, emerald, all of it fired in the city's famous ovens. Feathers may be added for effect. Time was, the old women removed their masks at night, in the dark, but now it is the law that they must wear them, even to sleep, even to dream. The hands must be gloved. The toes must be sheathed. The old women may be sixty or ninety, or two-hundred and ten. Despite their wild hues, no one sees them at all.

When Words Clung to Paper

The water rose slowly at first and then in a rush. This had happened so often that now we evacuated quickly, with maximum efficiency: children in hand, the papers stating our identity, laptops, cash, a few ragged photos, snacks.

Off we went, up the desolate peak to wait and complain. Days, weeks. New children were born. Time swam.

Nothing was drying.

Rain became snow, and the water was sealed with an icy crust. The city remained submerged.

※　※　※

By springtime, those who were judged to be physically fit were suited up with oxygen, with axes, with flippers and facemasks, to see what they could salvage. A powerful current flowed throughout the city. Remains floated past: suggestions of flesh, food, clothing, upholstery livid with rot, and life's little luxuries, books with words washed off.

It goes without saying, the old people couldn't manage this task. They were too brittle, too afflicted with nostalgia to be trusted. Really, the children were best at this. They were quickest at cracking and slipping through windows, a crevice, a hall, nimblest at grabbing this and that, eluding their flippering mothers. Men in their muscular prime held contests for speed and élan, breaking the surface, effulgent with news.

The city endured! Tall towers of commerce, their rooftop antennas hundreds of feet underwater, boardrooms sunk in muck and slime, were nevertheless remediable, the luxury condos (water views, all!), the domed and spired houses of worship, retail emporiums, theaters, the city's vast cities of the dead, angel and marble, the radial suburbs, why, even the hovels of the poor were bloated but whole, like castles for fish. The fish were dead, but this did not matter.

Our leaders convened. They reported that a plan had been hatched.

❉ ❉ ❉

The old folks would die on the desolate peak, dreaming of a long-lost— and frankly, mostly fictional—youth, but this could not be helped.

Oxygen was plentiful for everyone who chose to reside in the underwater city, embracing the future, partaking at the newly constructed municipal tanks.

Soon there were experts in aqueous disruption, and smart new metrics for business and life. In just a short while, we were told, we would develop new muscles, new skills, new habits of breathing. The children, of course, would be first to adapt. Every generation would continue to improve until the skin grew slick, until the blood grew cold, until the tanks were obsolete. The old ways would be completely forgotten. No one would recall when the city stood on land, when words clung to paper, when birds might be heard from afar.

The Second City (1933–34)

1. The Fan Dancer

In the beginning, the dancer used fans. The fans were made of feathers. The feathers were ostrich. So skilled was the dancer in moving the fans back and forth in front of her body that people believed she was naked beneath them.

This was an illusion, a trick of the eye.

In the beginning, the dancer was a classical performer who failed to earn a living. In the beginning, the dancer was a girl. In the beginning, the dancer was an egg. In the beginning, the dancer was seed. In the beginning, the dancer was weightless, unseeable, and boundless.

Never mind. The beginning makes no difference for the purpose of this story. The stage where this story takes place, where the dancer performed with her fans, was in "The Streets of Paris." The dancer was not French—not at the time of the story, nor in the beginning. The stage where this dance was performed was not in Paris, nor in France, nor in the streets, nor in Berlin with its famously risqué cabarets, nor in Brussels, or Vienna, or Warsaw, nor anywhere in Europe. In fact, "The Streets of Paris" could be found across an ocean, at the great world's fair called The Century of Progress. Over the course of a summer, millions of citizens crowded into temporary structures—which, in the beginning, had been nothing—to celebrate a vision of the future, and also to enjoy a bit of naughty entertainment.

Night after night, the dancer was arrested. Her ostrich-feather act was deemed indecent.

The following summer, The Century of Progress re-opened for its second and final season in Chicago. It was 1934. The feather-fans were gone but not the dancer. She had changed her act and was dancing in a bubble.

2. The Intended

The babies were in the machines in there, pristine behind glass.

The crowd pressed ahead.

"Will you look at them now," he said to me.

I looked at him. His damp brow. Dark eyes. The face filled with something other than wonder, it seemed to me. Rebuke, perhaps. Or grief. Maybe grief, come to think of it. The cut of the hair. A shadow, arid, under the flesh, the angle of the jaw that was familiar to me.

I had been here before—the halls, the lines, the spectacle of infant incubation, thrall of the heat. I thought everyone had, that second summer of the fair. The air smelled of perfume, of molten gardenia, and also of sweat.

There was a woman selling salt.

The babies were stirring ever so slightly, each in isolation.

"Imagine," he said.

Weight, breath: The nurses were jotting all the necessary factors.

I, of course, agreed with him, although I did not know what I'd agreed to.

Oh, what a fair! They called it the Century of Progress: a view of the future. Halfway to 1935, July in a curdle. The Sky Ride over the whole of the lakefront. Lights, sweets. The jewel on my finger. The heart of Chicago beating in the water, the world beneath our feet. We'd walked and walked. Kraft, Ford, Goodyear. The great halls of Science, of Travel and Transport; the Hall of Religion. The grand planetarium, catcher of starlight, revealing the heavens. Show homes constructed of prefabricated elements, a taste of the way we were to live.

And yet among wonders it came to this: the babies, for whom we stood in wait—the coiled line made faint with heat.

"Impossible," he said. Lungs unformed; the seen veins. And still they were breathing.

His hand was on my arm, in a manner of possession or possibly distress.

The doctor intended to save them all: these dreamers, translucent; these citizens in ovens.

Sailor, baker, mother, lover, captain of industry.

What were the odds?

Did I say that I was to marry this man?

We looked and then walked. It was required of us, and there was everybody waiting.

3. *The Double*

Out on the midway—alive!—not far from Midget City and the man made of rubber and the lady with the beard and the gent who could hammer a stake up his nose and the babies on display in incubation machines, was a young brown girl, little more than a baby, who upstaged them. The girl had been born with a highly unlikely condition, with additional limbs twisting out of her torso. Everyone involved made a beautiful profit. Her parents had twelve other children to feed. What else could they do with such a daughter, in 1934? To the crowds who were hungry to see her, it looked as if the little girl's body had been somehow mis-assembled, incompletely conjoined—as if she had another child inside her, faceless, craving escape.

Pre·fab·ri·cate

/prēˈfabrəˌkāt/

verb

past tense: prefabricated; past participle: prefabricated

1. Manufacture sections of something (especially a building or piece of furniture) to enable quick and easy assembly on site. "The homes at the Century of Progress were made of prefabricated elements."
2. Pre-manufacture the truth; conceive a lie in advance of an occasion.
3. Create imaginary people in order to house a pre-fabricated tale.
4. Construct imaginary cities in order to house a tale inside a person or persons imagined or real.

Atlas, Abridged

1. *The City of Infinite Names*

Everyone is lost here, even the mice. The old folks wander alone or in groups, searching for home, but the streets have new names, have turned in different directions. The city itself changes name every hour. At noon it is named for a saint. At one, a politician. At two it has a name in a language that cannot be spoken. Each day is different. Each minute is the same. Every iron statue, every monument identical. The earth smells of salt or of mouse or of blood—but no, that's not it.

The women wear keys at their throats like a necklace, but all of the doors have been burned to the ground, for they belong to a city that no longer exists.

2. *Under the Dirt*

Under the dirt lie the bones of the dead. They, too, are stateless.

3. *The City of Exits*

Every edifice in the city now known as the City of Exits has a door marked "out." No one is out. No one is in. The houses are vacant, the churches, the synagogues, temples, mosques, the old market, the hospital, brothels, streets. Bones shrink on dishes, flesh stripped off. There are shoes lost in haste. The gates are stuck open. The clocks have all stopped, each marking a different hour of depletion. Birds' nests are splintering cups holding nothing. Nobody knows where the souls of the City of Exits have gone. It is rumored they fled on a Tuesday, or maybe a Wednesday, or some other day named for some other god. It is rumored they are living in the City of Infinite Names.

4. Beyond the Edge of Memory

The night sky is crammed full of gods who've been forgotten. Light of the heavens, light of the past. The hunter never catches his prey, the glimmering dogs are toothless. Near Taurus, the Pleiades, seven nymph sisters are endlessly flirting, forever in suspension.

And who in your brilliant city even sees them? Who on your ravaged earth?

5. Hades

Persephone could tell you, that fistful of pomegranate seeds wasn't worth it. Ecstasy is fleeting. Night after night, she is biding her time in this darkness where even the dead have ambitions. And why would they not? Pride outlasts the body. Even self-loathing is a form of hubris.

6. The City of Holes

The holes are of varying widths and of untapped depths, a matrix of shimmering vacancies, great vaults of absence.

Every living being in the city of holes is held together and connected by holes. Captain of industry. Captain of air. Sailor, baker, mother, lover. Incubated baby and hesitant bride. Particle and element.

Bird. Nest.

A hole is not grief. A hole has no language. Yearning, you think, or possibility, but these are only words, with no home in a hole.

The holes in the city of holes cannot be filled by any nameable substance: solid, viscous, fluid, verbal, angel, feather, gas. A hole is not a color.

The city of holes is not a city, of course, which is why it has no limits.

The All-New Sanitary City

Sneezing is illegal in the Sanitary City. Also unlawful are sniffling, drooling, sweating, and sighing. Kissing! Verboten. All of the walls in the sanitary city are stainless, wiped on the hour. Sheets on the beds are made of paper, all the mattresses de-feathered. Many people come to the sanitary city for refuge from bodily fluid. Menstruation has been ended. Every insemination is mechanical. There is no fear in the sanitary city, no sorrow, no want, no unintended consequence. Nothing may swim from one life to another. Nothing may float from the breath to the ear.

Aquarium

"Think of it," the mother said, "as if it were a secret, hidden city underwater.

"Think of it," the mother said, "as if it were a moving sculpture in time."

The daughter said, "I think of it as fish."

✿　✿　✿

The fish in the gift shop are orange and stuffed. The daughter says she wants one.

The mother says, "Maybe."

The mother says, "We'll see."

The lunchroom is serving sustainable seafood and no plastic bottles and also no straws to go with no soda.

The mother and daughter keep saying the same things over and over, as if pre-arranged.

The mother tells the daughter, "You ought to pay attention."

The daughter tells the mother, "I am paying attention."

The mother retrieves a napkin (recycled) and mops up the liquid the daughter has spilled.

"Mom!" the daughter says.

"I said we'll see," the mother says.

✿　✿　✿

The daughter thinks the mother sees all the wrong things.

❉   ❉   ❉

"Think of it like pumps," the mother says, explaining the mechanism of gills, the counter-current exchange. She is handing the daughter her purchase after all.

"Stop," the daughter says. "You are always comparing one thing to another."

Many years later, after the mother stops breathing while asleep, the daughter will take apart this scene and recompose the whole thing.

"Why is that so bad?" the mother says.

One Thing Is Not the Same as Another

The women were given a drug to enable them to sleep while their babies floated in the womb.

Were the babies dreaming? That would be fantastical.

The women bore babies without any limbs.

The women were given a promising hormone.

The daughters grew tumors, but not until later.

The daughters could never give birth themselves.

The women were sedated, cut open, sewn up. They were instructed to relax.

Can you hear the body sing?

The women awoke to find their ovaries discarded, wombs cast off, and really, why not. What use for them now?

The blood is not a sea. Your eyes are not stars.

A pause is not pregnant.

The City of Salt

The City of Salt is crowded with so many pillars there is scarcely a path for a visitor to walk, should one ever come. Lot's wife is at the center of things, and well-preserved, despite a bit of crumbling, a few lost inches of height, a slight tremor when the wind blows wild. She is surrounded by souls who looked where they oughtn't: in corners, askance, between the sheets. Straight in the mirror. Under the bed. And who among all of us, really, has ever resisted to urge to look back?

The only thing to think about, incessantly, is fluid. But here you are:

A tree of dried life.

A desiccated garden, crystalline in sunlight.

Salted apple.

Sulfured plum.

Cured fig.

Brimstone.

Each and every pillar—short, tall, thick, thin, pregnant, or pinched—has her own exquisite shape, unlicked by either animal or lover, nor tongues of raging flame; no rotted flesh, no withered bone. And as for the heart—the heart is sentimental, and there is no sentiment in salt.

Conductivity

The second time she looked, the house was empty. Well, not of course empty. The mess. Husks. The stained sheets. The dinnerware. The bedding in ruins.

Liquid, or some sort of compound, she thought. To be productive was imperative.

The phone was not working.

Her face, which she'd looked at too much, did not please her, and still she continued to look at it.

Thieves came to the door and walked off with nothing.

The telephone man: a sensible person. This is why nobody listens to you, she thought he said.

Water, he said.

Water appeared in impossible places, saline stains.

Listen, she said.

The chairs, which were upholstered, repeated themselves. She tried one, then the other.

Her face, reconsidered, looked bloated to her. She would pull back the flesh. She would claw at the fabric, damage the arms, the interchangeable legs. She would interrogate the crystal.

Fork to the glass: It's ringing, she said.

Peacock

Mother saw it first, over by the hut. "See," she said, regarding us: sisters, offspring, preeners for love.

"Believe me," she said, but our gaze had gone yonder, in search of diversion, north, east.

We were travelers here. We had come for the air, for the view, for the natural aspect, Mother had said.

"The air will do you good," she said. "Careful your feet."

Regarding ourselves: There were dozens of us. Our hair was scented, piney, impeccably rinsed; our bodies bejeweled, beribboned, bedecked, in an affront to practicality.

The cold did not occur to us, the spewing of ash. We ran without shoes. Our toes were plump and painted. We sang through the trees, and our breath spun steam. "Can you hear us?" we trilled, one to the other. "Here! Here!"

The hut was strictly forbidden to us, Mother had said. We found our way in, in a crouch, on a lark; allowed our eyes to adjust. It was a skin with no one in it. Only us.

Mother was always nourishing something, wasn't she? Palms up, hands full, calling us—"Come, come"—bidding us, urging us, sizing us up.

She knew what we'd do.

Of course there were men, there were loves, there were sons, there were daughters we bore. Would you think there were not?

Our cries flew out throughout the hills in bliss and distress. The trees, grown heavy with snow, flung limbs.

We sang to our offspring, songs we remembered, skipping the words.

There were hundreds of us.

We lost our adornments, tore our bright garments, emptied our breasts. Swelled, drooped. Chipped, shed. Grew sweet and slack and fierce again. We shifted our shape. We boiled our voices. Our bellies were vacant, our nettled sex drawn.

The earth crackled under us; feet left prints. And still the wind blew.

Our babies, not children, nor listeners they—grown tall and lithe or sinewy, grown cheeky and willful—our babies created new uses for us.

Sitters, squatters, sibilant stewers—"Shhh!" we said.

The land was stripped.

The hut was disassembed and carried away when we were not present.

A cup fell and broke.

"No wonder," we said: Our hands were as birds'; no grip was left.

We held our own council.

Stars fell at night. The sky emerged brilliant. "Aurora," we said; we had anticipated this, though we saw only black and white. The Pleiades twinkled.

❋ ❋ ❋

And still the world was underfoot. And still the breeze carried a cry we remembered, or thought we did. Long after Mother was so long gone, when most of what remained of us was longing, our bones, we embarked upon a stroll. "Careful," we said, distrusting our hips. Our brittled feet moved us. Breath rose burnt. Wood was what awaited us, an unmarked grave. And still we persisted: Siblings, squinters, walkers in shadow, bundled recallers, benevolent—mostly benevolent—crones.

❋ ❋ ❋

The thing was iridescent, fanning itself. Nobody said, "See." It was impossible not to, caught in light: hundreds of eyes, the crest, the beak, uncelebrated body—earthbound home to the avian heart.

The Balloonist

There once was a man who lived in a county of a kingdom that no longer exists. At the center of the county was a castle which was ruined several centuries before the man was born.

The man was a painter, and also an astronomer, photographer, enjoyer of women, collector of weapons, traveler of continents. His thirst was for the world. It was a thirst that was unquenchable by land or by sea.

One day the man went up in a balloon, an envelope of air like a missive to the heavens. No one had seen such a thing in the kingdom. High above earth in his opulent basket, he waved in exhilaration and farewell.

Gravity, of course, is inescapable. In time, the man exhausted his fortune. Rather than be grounded, he shot himself to death.

The remains of the castle, which now belongs to another country, continues to be a tourist destination.

The Big Book of Elephants

The elephant keeper sat outside the elephant enclosure reading *The Big Book of Elephants*. The weather was perfect for such an endeavor, breezy, and not too warm, with a slight scent of elephant and hay. Given the three different species of *Elephantidae*, the elephant keeper had much to learn. *The Big Book of Elephants* was printed on glossy, oversized pages and had many illustrations of the species of elephant who live in the bush and in the forests of Africa and Asia as well as on midways and also in zoos and in other enclosures, such as the one that he, the elephant keeper, was guarding while eating a large bag of peanuts. The elephant keeper wore an ivory ring. He had a comfortable seat. He had a tall glass with ice. So deeply immersed was the elephant keeper in reading *The Big Book of Elephants* cover to cover, trunk to tail, that evening fell and the elephant keeper's glass was dry and his beard grew in and his nails grew long and his kids grew up and his wife ran off and his neighbors were rounded up and killed and his city's name was changed and the elephant enclosure was empty, all of which the elephant keeper failed to notice. He sat and continued to read, with a mountain of shells at his feet.

Far From the Sea

We lay in the tall grass, watching the sky, heavy with birds. Skin to reed, to blade, a green prickle. An itch.

We had nowhere to go.

Breeze, but just barely. The birds, which were geese, seemed mis-shapen, chemically plumped, their natures disrupted.

How many falls had we lain here together, scratching on earth we would one day lie under, under the sky. Did I say it was loud? "Listen," he said. Directive. A sentence. A place time goes.

Goddess, Un-enchanted

And so it came to pass that Daphne grew weary of being a tree. She'd had her fill of scabby humans scaling her limbs, and pissing dogs, and men denuding her branches for laurel wreaths with which to laud themselves. Young lovers cut into her bark, scarring her flesh with their impermanent affections. Sticky creatures tapped her sap, and witchy old women stripped her leaves to boil them for unguents.

The centuries ran rings around her heart. She sighed in the wind and she moaned to the moon and the stars, many of whom had also been nymphs back in the day.

Then came the rains. Then came the floods and the wind and the lashings, as never before. Was it, then, the livid moon, wild in her cycles, who riled the tides, swallowing city and forest and farm, knocking down walls, smashing the dams, severing roots—a violent answer to a ceaseless lament? Or was this the simple, logical consequence of centuries of progress?

And who on this earth, will grieve for a tree? Who will hear a forest fall?

Who, for that matter, will pass an ancient woman and recognize her beauty?

The City of Elms

I might have known her anywhere: the wreck of a cheek, the loose lid of an eye, the broken vein, felled breast, the burst cloud of the iris.

Tossing dirt: "The trees have something wrong with them. I think so," I said.

"I don't see it," she said.

The stones were carved with wings and such. Slab after slab.

She was missing an arm. Her hug was a half, and I wished to refuse her.

"Thirsty?" I said, as I pulled us apart.

"Famished," she said.

I said, "What are these made of?"

"Silk?" she said. "Might be something synthetic." Artificial daisies between us, sleeves on wood—mine: my hands, my broken nails, the dirt underneath them. Blood too.

Coffee with something else in it.

"Eggs agree with grief," I said.

"No yoke," she said. "My heart. I want only the white."

"I want bacon," I said.

"Something is in my eyes," she said.

Smears. Crumbs. The flesh I had not touched at all, wrinkled and stiffened.

"I still think . . ." I said to her.

She dabbed her face, rearranged the salt and pepper. I watched as she settled us up with the server. I said, "If you insist."

She might have insisted.

"It might have been fungus," I said to her. "The cause of death."

She fingered my plate. "Listen," she said. "Do you want this or not?"

The Art of Living in Advance

1. The mouth is saturated with the taste of something new

Wind is what wakes her, wind and rain, against the hotel window: he, in a slant across the king-sized bed, as if to fill the whole of it; she curled tightly, knees to chest. Nausea rolls up in her. Feet to the floor. Nose to the glass. The rain, she sees, in the light from the street, falls thickly, as if not entirely liquid. Across the street a flag is flapping madly.

She enters the bathroom and splashes her face. Reflected back: pale, slim, her face slightly bloated—younger, she thinks, than hours before, dressed up, made up: the luminous muse. Young as the daughter her lover doesn't have. The light has a flicker. The hotel he'd researched, meticulously. He likes to live in advance.

She tosses a washcloth. Walks back out and watches him breathe.

In the glow from the street, the spit of light from the bathroom, she tries out a password. Second pass. As it is in every fairytale, the third time's the charm.

2. "Travelers in Providence"

"Do you want to hear my idea?" he said.

She didn't, not really, not then. She was tired, having been up in the night. But it wasn't a question, anyway. His mind was his wealth (and her youth was hers). That's why she was with him, wasn't it? She craved his fame, however middling it was, his place at the table—and hers, someday. He wasn't one to fool himself (he told himself that; he took pride in being difficult to trick).

They had hours to kill. They had coffee and some kind of sticky tart. Café La France, the place was called, the concession in the station.

"You see," he said. "I am setting it here." His story, he meant, the work he'd been absorbed in, snappish and distant, but now on a high as a result of the gala the previous evening. His old alma mater, the theater packed. A triumph indeed—that woman had said so, clutching the volume he'd written, sweeping her hair back at the reception, feting him further, late at night, at the establishment the faculty favored.

"Here? Where?" She—the young and increasingly inappropriate lover—opened a sugar.

"Here in the station. Providence station. It's perfect for this story."

He was ever so slightly hung-over, she thought, with a check in his pocket, wind in his chest.

"Obviously, there are nuances. Subtexts. And matters will arise in the course of composition, but this is the gist . . ."

The rain had turned to snow by the time he had awakened a few hours earlier—wet, sloppy flakes that would soon begin to stick (the forecast was certain) and blanket the city and bring it to a halt. He'd worried aloud—delays, cancellations—he *had* to get back to The City (as if there was only one City) he said. This, he said, in his particular, sentence-splitting diction, was of utmost importance (meetings, etcetera, and while he was at it, his doddering mutt), and so they'd packed in haste: he, the ironic jacket and tie, thick books unread; she, the tiny hot pink dress, crushed now and dirty; her shoes spiked and strappy—utterly wrong, she had seen upon arriving (the way the gaze fell, the moneyed tone of the voice), toothpaste, pills for a headache, gum, her birth control not recently opened, soaps she had swiped. He was in jeans now and she in dark leggings, a shirt that was his and was huge on her. "Swimming," she said, with satisfaction in her voice.

Down in the lobby, past "Aspire," the restaurant which featured a fish tank—"We'd better move quickly," he'd said to her. "Let's try to get out on an earlier train."

Business, pleasure: Checkout was crowded. A mother and daughter (not much younger, it seemed, than the lover). "Mom!" the daughter said. "Must you always repeat?"

"Taxi," he said.

"Train," he said.

"Crap," he said. "This is exactly, precisely, just what I didn't need to have happen."

❁ ❁ ❁

"So here's the idea," he said to her. Their train was late, and no, there was not a single seat, not one (although there were two of them traveling together), on the earlier train. Sold out. Completely. He'd asked more than once.

"It's snowing," he said.

"I know," she said. "Oh, you mean in the story?"

"Obviously. The story is what I am talking about. It's snowing hard, the light is strange, and this young fellow—college man, he's maybe a senior, handsome, lucky, you know the type—he is waiting at the station to pick up this girl."

"Girl?"

"Okay, woman. This *woman*. Louise is her name. I am naming her that, Louise, I think. I like the liquidy "l". She, Louise, is returning to him on the train from The City. But due to the weather . . ."

"Right," she said. Café la France was crowded. Latte quaffers. Girls eating yogurt. A toddler—God spare them, she thought. At least they had seats.

"I already had the idea," he said. "Before this trip. That's what's strange. The train, the snow. The man, I haven't named him yet, but you know, someone-the-third. Drives a nice car."

"Benz?" she said.

"Maybe," he said. "He'd driven Louise here a few days before, to the station—outbound, her train to The City, for a short trip. But this is the thing: She didn't tell him, precisely, where she was going or why she was going, details and reasons, this girl, this *woman* of his. He hadn't really asked. She did this sometimes, flitted off, the years they'd been together—three, I think. Yes, three it is. But this last time she'd looked so sad, so slumped, he thought, so thin yet somehow puffy, her long curls spilling—her face, sad and desolate, her eyes . . . She'd worn a pink coat. She was going away, for just a few days . . . and of course he had a car; he had driven her here, to the station. He knew he hadn't wanted to look at her sadness. It angered him slightly. And he, too, was sad—yes, he was, because he knew he had to end it."

He waited for the question, begging for it.

"End it," he said.

"Why," she said, to move it along.

"Why?" he said, as if surprised she had asked. "Because for all that he loved her, for all that she *knew* him—you know, knew that he wanted, for instance, to . . . act, to perform, and not be the . . . let's see, *lawyer* his father expected, for all they had dreamed, their romance could not last. His parents would insist, of course, subtly, but still . . . His father, his mother, the family name . . . Louise was inappropriate . . . smart and ambitious, but still, there was a matter of—let's say religion, and, well, *ilk*."

"Ilk?" she said.

"Don't sulk," he said. "You know what I mean. And this is in the past, I said. Didn't I say? Late 70s. I had to have mentioned that, no?"

"No," she said. "You didn't."

"It wasn't so easy for him," he said.

"Really?" she said.

"Little you know. Free love and such, the way the world was changing, all of it changing—sure, of course. But not for him. Louise had to go. Louise could not last. He knows that, accepts that, the way it has to be, and he knows that it ought to end sooner than later—as soon as she returns!—and also he knows that she knows that too. Of course she does. She's smart, Louise. And now at the station, he is waiting for her, and he is filled with trepidation, drowning in anxiety, waiting and waiting, and so upset—the train is delayed, the station looks strange, looks wrong, transformed, not the way he recalls it, not how he thought of the place at all. Nothing's as it used to be. He's shaking. And also, despite that it's crowded—the station is not that big to begin with, round, domed, and now it is packed full of families and youth, the art kids with sketchpads, women in pairs, the men in suits, you know—everyone gives him a sort of berth, as if maybe they don't want to brush up against him. As if he stinks. As if, he thinks, it's the sadness he feels, the strangeness he feels. He is tired, too. He goes to get coffee but doesn't remember the coffee being expensive like this, fancy like this, and he doesn't have cash, or not enough, not on him. The girl—the woman—at the register is looking at him, as if he doesn't understand, as if he doesn't belong there. He doesn't much like that. And so he walks away again. He sits on the floor, against a wall, that wall, that one over there—the seats, every one of them, taken, you see. The board keeps rolling, more delays. Coming in increments. Later, later. Snow keeps falling, feathery at first and thicker now, according to the chatter of the people around him, muffled as it is. He—from where he is—can't see. He starts to sleep. He sleeps. He starts to dream in his sleep. He is possibly even snoring a little, there on the floor. And this is the dream: The dream is the future. His future self. And he is entering a house like the house he grew up in, similar in stateliness, silver and oak, the foreseeable children—a girl and a boy. He has a brief-case in hand. There is a weight in his heart, and from another room he can hear a woman speaking, maybe on the telephone—yes, on the telephone, and then he sees the woman, the one who is his wife. And she is not, of course, Louise, of course she's not, and he is suddenly flooded, there in the dream, with a bone-chilling sadness, a wave of emotion that makes him ache. He wakes up on the floor."

"Are you sure you don't want a bite of this pastry?"

"No," he said, peevish. "Listen. As I was saying . . . Well, maybe. A taste."

"What then?" she said.

"Not bad," he said, brushing a crumb off. "A little too sweet. So there he is sitting, waiting, filled with this sadness, and that's when it hits him: She might have been pregnant! That must have been it . . . she went to The City, Louise—why else, what for? And of course it was his, his child, his flesh and blood, and how could he not have known it before? He vows on the spot to propose to Louise, to marry Louise, throw it all to the wind, take heed of the dream, the message, if only it's not too late . . . you know . . ."

"I get it," she said. "But why did she need to travel to The City? It wasn't illegal, was it then?"

He made a motion with his hand as if to swat away the question. Logistics, for all of his forethought, annoyed him; she knew that well. "I'll figure it out," he said to her. "That isn't the point. So anyway, the train at last is coming, it's coming at last; and filled with resolve, he waits by the tracks. He goes down to the tracks. Track Two. A clot of people. Confusing. The looks he gets, as if he is dirty—why, he can't fathom. The train comes in, the one heading north, and people pile off. Rush off. Parents and children, their coats and their bundles, their baggage, their breath . . . it's cold down there and snow falls hard, he can see it from the platform. And then . . . there at the end of the platform, the girl at the edge of his vision is her, Louise, a little bit ghostly in a pink coat, but only for a moment. And then: She is gone. He simply can't find her. He looks and he looks. The train is pulling out again . . ."

She swallowed her latte. Looked at her watch, which was always fast, which she always forgot for a minute or two.

"And then he reconsiders. He must have been mistaken. He must have been confused. She must be on the next train. She must have told him something. She must have missed her train—they didn't have cell phones, not back then."

"I know that," she said.

"He simply has to wait, he thinks. He sits on the bench now, a seat newly vacant. He's tired, so tired. The room seems strange. And then he falls asleep again. I think he falls asleep again, waiting, and feels her, Louise, her arm around his shoulder, her presence, there as if to comfort him, as if to forgive him, and then . . ."

"Then?"

"The trains come and go, come and go. The light dies. At last it is the last scheduled train of the day that's arriving. Announced on the speaker. Track two."

Crowded around them were people holding their coffees, their yogurts, their muffins, waiting to sit. She did not interrupt him.

"He gets off the bench now and goes down the stairs, descends, so cold, so tired, track two, and snow is still falling, falling . . . There she is! Yes, there she is! But dressed wrong, somehow, there amid the passengers coming off the train, and the shape of her body, and then her face, her eyes . . . Not her. He heaves an awful sigh and his breath fills the air. And he looks in the windows, looks in a door but the train is on the move again, onward. Onward."

She heard how his voice was filled with emotion, despite his cultivation of dispassion.

"Back in the station, he looks and he looks, by the newsstand, distraught, and out by the taxis . . . and then . . ."

"Then?"

"The ladies'! She must have gone in there. He ought to have known. Of course! That's it! He goes and he opens the ladies' room door, and a woman yells, 'Hey! Hey, Mister! What do you think you're doing here?' And here come the cops."

"Police?" she said. "There in the station?"

"Well, station personnel," he said. "Really. Whatever. The point is, they take him by the arm, they've come to take him away, but just for a moment he catches a glimpse of a ravaged old man in the ladies' room mirror. 'Come, you have to leave now,' the cop or the guard or whoever he is, says, shooing him out. 'You know you can't be here.'

" 'Louise!' he cries. 'Louise! Louise!' And he is out on the street."

People were listening in on them.

His voice was raised: " 'The poor old soul,' the second guard—he's worked there longer—says to the first. 'Whenever it snows like this, he's here.' He shakes his head, the guard does. 'Somebody told me he once was a lawyer. Lost his mind. That girl died 30 years ago," the guard says. "Before the new station—back when the train stopped south of here. They say the girl jumped—to the tracks. Track two.' "

"She jumped?"

He looked at her, expectant.

"That's it?" she said.

"That's it," he said. "The point is he's guilty. He killed her. Okay, he didn't push her, at least, I don't think so; it's still his fault. He is crazy from guilt, regret that was dormant for much of his life."

"*You* killed her," she said.

"Oh, please," he said.

"You wrote it," she said. "You got rid of the girl. The *woman*."

"Come on," he said. "Don't be like that. You really don't get it."

"What should I get? Do you want me to like him? Is that it? Forgive him? Feel sorry for him? And anyway, this story," she said (she simply couldn't help herself—she knew she shouldn't say it, she ought to let it go, she always did, but the woman last night at the reading, the way she was carrying on and on . . .),"it doesn't make sense. I mean, the timing is wrong."

"I know the timing is wrong. He . . ."

"No," she said. "The story. If this, this tale of Louise, was in the 70s, he's . . . your age. Not so old. Not yet. Not old enough yet to have dementia like that, to be ravaged like that."

"But he's crazy," he said. He crumpled his napkin. "I guess you have a point, maybe literally speaking. But listen. Maybe the framing is different. The fifties or something. The time doesn't matter. Or, I know. Maybe—he might have had a stroke."

"Now, why would he have a stroke?" she said.

"An addiction," he said.

"We ought to give up our table," she said. "All of these people are waiting to sit."

✳ ✳ ✳

"So who was she, really? Louise," she said. "You based her on someone."

"No one," he said.

She turned away.

"Don't do this," he said.

"She had to be someone. Everyone you write about is someone you know. And why would you tell me a story like that?" The snow was a cliché, she thought. He ought to know better and probably did. So what was his point?

They stood by the time board—every seat taken under the dome— as new delays clicked into view. "For God's sake, let it go," he said.

The air froze between them, an interstice in consciousness.

She could see the future; she didn't need to dream it. Sooner or later the train would come. The laws of things. The two of them grasping their bags, boarding the train, claiming their places. Each would read, or fake it. Back in The City, they'd stop for a drink. They would laugh over nothing. Make it up, brush it off. Neither of them would speak of the story ever again, though later he would publish it. Nevertheless, for the rest of the time they were lovers (which wouldn't be very much longer—she'd ceased to adore him—plus, the other woman was planning to call) *Louise* would disturb them. Whoever she'd been, whatever she'd done, whatever her significance, for them, she was real and could not be uninvented.

He knew what he was doing.

"People you've known for a very short while will stay with you always," he'd said to her once. "Regret. Impossibility. That's something you don't understand yet..."

3. The Art of Living in Advance

She turns off his laptop, there in the dark. His name is his password. First. Last. Crackable. Practical precautions—he isn't very good at them (she tells herself that), for all of his planning, for all of his critically acclaimed self-awareness. She'd read the thing twice. "Travelers in Providence," modified the day before, on the train up here. (And in parens: or maybe "Gestation").

The action she's taken cannot be reversed.

He murmurs in sleep as she lies down beside him, nose to nape.

Soon he'll awaken. Soon he will worry (delays, cancellations). Soon they will go to the station and quibble. This, that. (Although it isn't Providence. It's somewhere much colder, and windier too.) He will state his idea at breakfast, the plot.

The future he can't correctly imagine, for all that he tries.

"Listen," he'll say.

"It's snowing . . ." he'll say.

They will enter the train. He will answer a text. She will swallow a pill, which will cause her to bleed. He will type in his name: first, last. She will plead an excuse. He will click on a file. She will change her seat, before he apprehends that it is she, Louise, who has deleted the body.

The Lost City

The City of Endless Reflection

Every mirrored surface in the City of Endless Reflection is meticulously covered, in keeping with the sacred custom following a death. Walls, doors, the ceiling, even the mirrored fixtures, the floor, the books silvered with wisdom, are draped.

You know what you look like anyway. You tell yourself this, as you examine your eyes in the blade of a knife. The knife is not clean. It has a residue of egg.

The mirrored table has been clothed, the plates have been professionally scraped to dull their shimmer, the forks and the spoons have been coated in an agent specifically created for mourning, but someone in the rapture of grief has neglected this single utensil.

Owing to this regrettable lapse, you are forever condemned to see yourself in everything, distorted, occluded, everywhere you look.

Your Mouth Is a Shroud

Your mouth is a shroud. If you could you would swallow yourself.

The Lover

Her lover built a castle, but only of words. Her lover was her lover in spirit, on paper, in mind, in heart, but not in the flesh.

Her lover coughed. Her lover turned one thing into another, fantastical, contorted, tortured. He was endlessly creating impossible scenarios, horrifying rules. Her lover died at 40, in a sanatorium outside of Vienna.

The cause was consumption. By then they'd been estranged, although their love appeared to linger.

Twenty years later, in a setting with a beautiful name, not far from Berlin, in a town until then most noted for its palace, she quietly expired. The cause was the kidneys. The cause was starvation, exhaustion, the penetrating cold, the lack of medical attention. The cause was words. She was guilty of those, and her name had been replaced with a number. The cause was deeds, smuggling out the living, in defiance of the ruling regime. The cause was sticking out her neck. The cause was that she loved. The cause was that the body, made of flesh, had ceased to breathe.

Saviors

1. His Life in My Hands

Everything I loved was in the water. The sky overturned, his life in my hands, me towing him through another element, a ripple. The world an open mouth.

People said we looked alike, and maybe we did. But I was the swimmer, and stronger. He knew it. I understood the undertow.

After that summer, it was never the same.

Some people don't want to be saved.

2. Plunge

Slowly, slowly, slowly, she said, and because we were both in the boat, I was listening up.

Feet on the gunwales, hands on hips, the thrill of postponement.

Pollen and something else in the breeze. Sand tamped in the hull. A fire lit somewhere for somebody else.

She was always steadier. Shorts and a half-top, blistered and sunburned. A squinter. Toe-dipper. Upholder of rules.

She said what she said as if she knew that the thing that would kill her was already in her.

Don't, she said.

3. In Defense of Preservation

Out at the lighthouse, breakers rose and broke over concrete that shouldn't have been there—ask us, please.

"It used to be natural rock," she said. She knew that I knew it.

Nights we'd jumped, in love with *no trespass*. Jagged in water. The rush to the lookout was grievous for mothers and casual drunks.

BOUNDLESS AS THE SKY

Look at us: too old to be orphans. Which we were, nonetheless. Ragged-eyed.

They'd covered it over. The color was oyster or possibly bone. It was all about progress and civic convenience.

"Awful, this," she said to me.

Up the hill a mile north, the bulk of our lovers were buried in dirt.

Spray hit the surface. Her face, in light, faded. Our sneakers were mottled.

"Which do you miss the most?" I said.

"Of what?" she said.

"My shoes are a disgrace," I said.

"They'll dry," she said. "The falling, I think. The possibility of it."

Pre·serve

/prə'zərv/

Noun

1. A sphere of activity reserved for a particular person or group or classification of persons ("flight is the preserve of those who are qualified or otherwise enabled to travel through air") typically those of a certain educational background, stature, gender, class, or genetic heritage.
2. A place where various types of animals are protected, sometimes for the purpose of killing them.
3. A sweet treat.

Verb

1. To maintain, protect or keep something in existence past its natural expiration, such as edible commodities; or alternately, documents and/or images and/or artifacts held by an institution, sometimes under climate-controlled conditions; or alternately, a physical body, such as a hunted animal, by means of an art which is the preserve of those certified in taxidermy; or alternately, a living human body, by means of naturally occurring and/or artificially created supplements and treatments and cosmetic toxins and/or masking, and subsequently, post-mortem, by means of more durable masking and/or embalming and entombment, which is the preserve of those who are licensed in such matters; or alternately, a body of knowledge, retained by means of words, which may be sung, spoken, written, or silently recited until forgotten.

The City Where Dogs Lie Dreaming

The dogs are the property of everyone and no one. The color of dust, the color of moon, the parched white of clay, they sprawl on the sidewalks panting in July, requiring pedestrians to sidestep. They lick at the fountains of the city's glory, eat from the hand, lie underneath the tables at the outdoor cafes, show their bellies to the sky. They wait for whatever will fall to fall.

In the old part of town, on narrow, coiled streets, up the hill that holds the churches, the old Jewish quarter, the stalls selling powders, and wine, and bread, the famed tiled baths, they are bloated with sleep, or watchful, discerning.

Pockets of the city hold monuments to souls who have departed. Cemeteries, yes, with their un-desecrated hush, but also the city's busiest circles, where the dead survey traffic and commerce from high upon their pedestals. The Mother of this country, with wine and with sword, is mythical and therefore immortal. Entombed in the museum is a glimpse of the vanished, the silenced, the scientists and artists, the writers and seekers—enemies, all, of an occupying state which no longer exists, from a century quickly receding from memory, along with a world that will never be born.

The dogs' ears are tagged. They are inoculated. Known. Whole hordes raise their voices in anticipation, for here comes a man whose punctuality a dog can set its heart by. Later, sated at the mouth of the glassy galleria where tourists in bhurkas or bright cotton dresses escape from the heat, the dogs lie dreaming what dreams dogs dream. Perhaps they are dreaming of you.

Where Graves Have No Names

In a city in Europe, a cemetery holds only stones, with no coffins, no bodies beneath them. The stones were re-homed in order to make the original graveyard a field for athletics. For reasons of efficiency, perhaps, or decorum, or sanitary practices, officials of the city in question decided to leave bodies interred. Now children kick balls over bones of the dead.

There is no map, no key to the cemetery holding no coffins. Some stones are polished, carved with the letters of a language no longer in use. Some stones are wordless markers of grief. And what of the pebbles, the feathers, the bent blades of grass?

Shadowplay

1. Visitation

I saw you again
    last night.
    You were smoking
    a cigarette, which you never did in life. Your dog
    seemed to know me.
    Nobody spoke.
    I wanted
    to linger,
    far from the firm, unyielding world of mattress, skin, walls, facts,
    the knock
    on the door that would not come,
    the caw
    of the living day.

2. Conversation

The women in this many-storied city have their tongues cut out. The lips of the women make shapes, but no sound emerges, not even a moan. At a certain time of day, when conditions are right, the women are enormous, covering sidewalks, houses, municipal structures, blanketing the streets, merging their aspects in seditious elision. They, among themselves, are completely understood.

3. Gestation

Nascent in the swelling belly of the earth, beneath the skin of stone and steel, beneath the living and the dead, beneath the steam and the smoke, beneath the river of rock, beneath the shell of liquid mineral, as hot as any sun or inferno, where no shade falls, lies a ball of solid iron, under pressure too high for it ever to melt.

The Uses of Fire on Earth

1. Prometheus's Eagle

How many times must he endure these deathless screams, ingest the bruised fruit of this organ? Truth be told, the eagle did not much care for the taste. Oh, for a bird, a fish, a bloody heart!

Days, the eagle gorged, as demanded, hungry and not.

Nights, the eagle soared, unable to rest, and thus observed mortals warming their haunches, stripping the roasted flesh off bones, igniting their torches, welding their weapons, blasting their cannons, building their bilious cities in order, it seemed, to name and rename and incinerate them and then do it again. They burnt humans at stake. Shot rockets from their scorched earth, in search of someplace else. They lit tapers in prayer, remembrance, supplication.

High up a mountain, free of the stench, the eagle, drunk on altitude and iron, encountered snow and ice, which in the light of the sun, appeared to him as fire, liquid and blinding, as if there had only ever been a single element. The eagle longed to linger, but could not.

He was bound to the tortured god who lay in wait.

2. Crematorium, and Eight More Words that Rhyme with It, Presented in Alphabetical Order

i. Auditorium

[aw-di-**tawr**-ee-*uh* m]

A place to present ideas, information, experiences, awards, and ideologies to large numbers of people. Such a presentation might center on the accomplishments of the past (progress) and/or the goals and technological wonders of a future to come (projected progress). It might involve social and political rhetoric, or matters entirely unrelated. A planetarium, for instance, frequently contains an auditorium in which the constellations are depicted on the ceiling, while an aquarium, to name another instance, might include an outdoor theatrical space for viewing living creatures trained to perform on command.

ii. Cafetorium

[kaf-i-**tawr**-ee-*uh* m]

An auditorium in which one may also mass-consume mass-produced food and fluid along with information, entertainment, and ideas, ingesting them simultaneously.

iii. Crematorium

[kree-m*uh*-**tawr**-ee-*uh* m]

A place where human bodies are incinerated. Cremation may involve sacred ritual, in which case, the burning of the body may be visible to mourners. Alternately, cremation may be achieved discretely, either for individual corpses or for large numbers of persons whose demise has resulted from, say, gas, ingested simultaneously, in consideration of scientific progress. Smoke from a crematorium may be seen from some distance, but the noise of cremation, such as the popping of the lungs, will not be heard through the thick walls.

iv. Emporium

[em-**pawr**-ee-*uh* m]

A marketplace, generally of products rather than ideologies. An emporium may typically sell clothing or furnishings or spices or flesh.

v. In Memoriam

[in m*uh*-**mawr**-ee-*uh* m]

A remembrance of a person or persons or class of persons deceased, owing to any number of causes. These may include the failure of vital organs such as the liver, kidneys or heart, the replication of pathogens and contagions, starvation, hypothermia, bullet wounds, knife wounds, asphyxiation due to fire or strangulation or drowning or gas, crimes of commerce or of passion or of both, simultaneously, age. Any *in memoriam* is an attempt at preservation and is dependent on memory, documentation, and language. Such language may be (and often is) subject to commercial production and may be disseminated electronically.

vi. Moratorium

[mawr-*uh*-**tawr**-ee-*uh* m]

A temporary cessation of activities or hostilities, lasting for a few minutes or a few hundred years, but with the assumption that such activities or hostilities will resume.

vii. Natatorium

[ney-t*uh*-**tawr**-ee-*uh* m]

A swimming pool, usually indoors.

viii. Sanatorium

[san-*uh*-**tawr**-ee-*uh* m]

A wellness spa or resort (now obsolete) for patients suffering from chronic conditions and diseases such as tuberculosis (consumption). Treatment included fresh air, healing waters, and rest, with outcomes that were at best uncertain. Some sanatoriums, however, were, in fact, "asylums" for individuals, including children, diagnosed with insanity, instability, disagreeability, and a variety of other unpleasant defects and perceived deficiencies impeding progress. Treatment included electric shock, insulin, sterilization, and starvation while tied to a bed, which achieved its intended result.

ix. Sudatorium

[soo-d*uh*-**tawr**-ee-*uh* m]

A Roman vaulted sweating room, hot air bath utilizing intense heat for the purpose of cleansing.

3. Burning Bush

God may have chosen to appear here, although scholars disagree as to whether the bush was in fact a bush, or the bush was merely brambles, or alternately, whether the bush was Mt. Sinai itself, as well as whether the fire was flame or whether the fire was pure light, as well as whose voice it was that Moses claimed to have heard. Regardless of such ongoing discordances, the discerning homeowner seeking to create a pop of color on his property does well to cultivate his own burning bush (*Euonymus alatus*). This sturdy crimson plant will thrive in many types of soil, requiring a minimum care, and offering visual pleasure for many generations to come.

The Penultimate City

Everything living and dead, solid and conjured, fruitful and not, has been wired together within and without this spectacular city in a feat of automation. Socket and plug. Tunnel and lock. Wine-dark sea and crenellated tower. Spray, wave, salt, root. Sailor, baker, mother, lover. Resin and sparkle. The apple and the hand are inextricably connected, ripe with intention. Sentient creatures of every disposition may be summoned or created or unmade by the sound of a voice, by the blink of an eye, by the flip of a switch, by an indolent sneeze, by the tap of a richly bejeweled toe, by a fleeting desire. Pieces of the past, such as love affairs or floods or conversations may be simply reconstructed or exchanged. Wars may be waged in reverse, the future recomposed. The weather may be simulated. Bodies may decay and be replaced, in whole or in part, or reconceived or discarded: aqueous, avian, earthbound. Celestial. Rain will continue to fall on the penultimate city. Light will continue to runnel through the cracks of its engineered streets, the crumbled ruins of its walls. The sky and the sea, and even the stones are made to breathe.

[Interlude]

PART TWO

BOUNDLESS AS THE SKY

You are a man, or haven't you heard
That you keep on trying to be a bird?

—W.H. Auden, *Journal of an Airman*

Balbo Here This Afternoon

24 Seaplanes Flying Today from Montreal
Army Flyers to Act as Escort

By Philip Kinsley

Italy's air armada of twenty-four seaplanes and 100 [sic] men will arrive in Chicago this afternoon, ending its epochal 7,000 mile flight from Rome to A Century of Progress. Last night, as the flyers rested in Montreal, their last stop before Chicago, leaders here had completed plans for a glorious welcome.

Gen. Italo Balbo, youthful commander of the fleet, is expected to lead his planes into the city between 3 and 5 o'clock this afternoon . . . The exact hour of arrival is necessarily uncertain.

—*The Chicago Tribune*, page one, Saturday, July 15, 1933

Streamers and Signs

Shhh. Quiet.

High overhead, the Sky Ride is empty. The aerial cars hang vacant, inert. Birds perch on a few. In the heat of the day and in the sizzle of the night, thousands of people will rise above Chicago, the city's gritty industry, the World's Fair ("The Century of Progress"), the Great Lake, with views stretching north to Wisconsin and south to Indiana, the sweat and heavy perfume of one another's bodies. Salt, breath.

Not yet. It is 5:29 a.m. (Chicago time) and the sun is just up. In this soft hour, there is nobody here, save *them*, the ones who will slip like a shadow through a gate, who will shelter in doorways, couple in the alleyways behind the exhibition halls, fight with the rats for an edible bite.

Close to the shoreline, the great halls and foreign pavilions, the domed Fort Dearborn (built, burnt down, re-built, and abandoned in the previous century, now reassembled as a replica, impenetrable as a fortress at night), the salt-and-ketchup restaurants (locked, their scraps well-picked), the midway, and the children's Enchanted Island are desolate, quiet. The art deco lights have gone dark and will not be rekindled till nightfall.

A light wind blows.

A watchdog is dreaming.

Shhh.

Someone is always awake in the infant incubator exhibition on the midway, the barely-there babies who live in the machines, and with them, a handful of sturdy nurses. The European doctor and his wife may be astir, air conditioning humming in their quarters on the premises. (The stew they have left outside, strategically placed for the taking, is gone, long gone, just a redolent stain; it is always the best of the fair, richer even than the leavings of the Café de Alex.) Directly behind this exhibit, you will find the Streets of Paris. The ladies who dance there, foremost among them Sally Rand with her big white fans, are finally sleeping. (There is never much of anything of worth outside her trailer).

Down the stretch, in Midget City, the self-appointed mayor is sipping hot tea outside, as he does every daybreak, his solitary interlude before his tiny wife and the whole of their tiny city arises. (Their trash is a gold mine, already dredged.)

Past the Midget City limits, in her trailer, the bearded lady snores and can be heard through the walls. Possibly, the fire-eater yawns on his mattress, burning through the thin tube of consciousness connecting sleep and waking.

And now comes the time to raise the shade on the city, the real one, cupping the Century of Progress, a perishable prize, in its hand. To the north, up the Gold Coast, from Rush Street to Oak, men and women of means and of high social station repose, for the most part, unruffled in bed; it is, after all, Saturday; tonight will run late. Their maids are afoot. In his stately residence, Rufus C. Dawes, the fair's President, is already dressing, wondering where in the devil is his watch; it's been missing for days. A mile away, Maj. Reed Landis, in charge of the reception committee for the fleet, is anxiously pacing his parquet floor.

All throughout the city, taxis and buses and elevated trains rumble onward, more than half-empty at this early hour, yet full of direction. The police are on alert. There was mayhem last night in some of the neighborhoods, revelry ending in broken glass. And now with the threats, the abductions for ransom, the con-men who prey on the Century of Progress, the vice squad complaints, it is all hands on deck, an eye in every corner (and sometimes a wink, a bill slipped in the hand). This much is clear: There must not be an incident today.

Down by the river at the *Tribune*, the presses are hot. Further to the South, in Hyde Park, the slumbering families may or may not be observing the Sabbath. In the old German neighborhood, Lincoln Park, a young man is stashing all his money in his wallet. Near West, in Little Italy, every porch and edifice is covered in streamers and signs, red, white, and green, the walls bursting with pride.

(Meanwhile, in another time zone, Gen. Italo Balbo is sweating, smoking, pouring a generous helping of cognac into his strong French brew. Today will reflect on Il Duce, as he has been warned again and again, as if he didn't know it. The airborne armada will land or die trying, in perfect formation. There can be no hesitation or mistake.)

In the cavernous kitchens of the Drake Hotel, where Landis and Dawes will preside at this evening's official festivities for everyone who matters (assuming, please God, that Balbo and all of his men arrive intact), the pastries and cakes are rising in the ovens. In the Drake's dank bowels, the laundresses are sanitizing sheets for future use, washing out the evidence of sleep and of sex. In its glittering lobby, the porters are rolling gold carts full of luggage.

And in the city's slaughterhouses, far to the west, doomed animals cower, as they always have.

"Shake a Leg!"

Jay Gold, Future Pilot, Newly-Licensed Ham Radio Operator and General Mastermind

Yes! He'd managed to grab the *Trib before* his father got hold of it. His father would wrinkle the paper for an hour over prune juice and margarine-toast, cut in quarters. Every morning, awful news from Germany, including today, Jay had to admit, in the column on the left. The seizure of fortunes of "enemies of state." *Your father is beside himself*, his mother would say. *Unconscionable*, his father would say, *criminal* and *evil*. Although it was only a matter of time before everyone came to their senses, his father would daily conclude and his mother would concur and Dessie would stare out the window or worse, play her gloomy music on the half-grand piano that took up half the living room and someone would discover that Brownie had once again piddled in the hallway and then of course Dessie would say it was *his* fault, that *her* job was watering the plants that were always dying anyway, and *can't we at least have some goddamned butter*, his father would say, until his mother said, *stop*.

Not today. Today was aviation history! The airborne Italian armada was coming! At last! And more: Already this morning, the one-eyed pilot Wiley Post had started his round-the-world solo, from Floyd Bennet Field in Brooklyn, New York. At this precise moment, he was already up there, soaring through air.

Here was the question: Could Post beat his previous round-the-world record? Jay and his cousin Morris who called himself Ace held discussions at night, in Morse Code, whole conversations in dashes and dots, on their home-made ham radios, skillfully assembled with vacuum tubes and oscillators, absolute necessities for any future pilot.

Jay could recite every detail regarding Post's flight:

Aircraft: Lockheed, white-and-purple monoplane.

Name: Winnie Mae.

Previous round-the-world record: 8 days, 15 hours, and 51 minutes, set by Post.

Previous co-pilot: Harold Getty.

Co-pilot this time: None. Only instruments.

Expert assessment: The flight speed (170 miles per hour) could increase due to strong west winds.

Problem: There was pressure off New York, and Post would have to deal with that.

Verdict: Time will tell.

Today's banner headline, obviously, was the impending arrival of the airborne armada. Even Wiley Post took a back seat for this, because never before had the world seen a feat of aviation as spectacular and risky. President Roosevelt was planning a tickertape parade in New York for later in the week. But first and most important was the landing in Chicago. *The Trib* had the log of every stop and every matter of significance concerning the fleet (well, except for the accident that killed a man in Amsterdam and broke up a plane on the very first leg, and then the terrible week when they were they were grounded in Iceland, but that was done and past).

. . . From Italy to America, Chicago time:

Friday, June 30—11:45 p.m. left Ortebello [sic], Italy.

Saturday, July 1—6:36 a.m. arrived Amsterdam, Holland. Distance from Ortebello [sic], 735 miles. Time, 6 hours, 51 minutes. Average speed, 106.8 mph.

Sunday, July 2—1:14 a.m. left Amsterdam. 5:25 a.m. arrived Londonderry, Ireland. Distance, 650 miles. Time, 4 hours 11 minutes. Average speed, 154.8 mph.

Wednesday, July 5—6:40 a.m., left Londonderry, Ireland. 1:15 p.m. landed at Reykjavik, Iceland. Distance, 930 miles. Time, 6 hours, 35 minutes. Average speed, 141 mph.

Wednesday, July 12— 2 a.m. left Reykjavik, Iceland. 1:50 p.m. landed at Cartwright, Labrador. Distance, 1500 miles. Time, 11 hours, 50 minutes. Average speed, 126.6 mph.

Thursday, July 13—8:20 a.m. left Cartwright, Labrador. 2:37 p.m. landed at Shediac, New Brunswick. Distance, 800 miles. Time, 6 hours, 17 minutes. Average speed, 127.2 mph.

Friday, July 14—8:52 a.m. left Shediac, New Brunswick. 12:51 p.m. landed at Montreal, Canada. Distance, 500 miles. Time, 3 hours, 51 minutes. Average speed, 125.6 mph.

Hundreds of thousands of people would wait at the lakefront and south at Soldier's Field to witness the arrival. Balbo would circle from the southwest direction of Gary, Indiana. Jay knew exactly which way to look. He had pilfered his father's off-limits binoculars to share with Ace, along with three dollar bills which he'd taken from his mother's dresser drawer where she hid her own money, plus a few quarters his father had neglected. Late last night, he and Ace had made a plan. Dot, dot, dash. Early that morning, he had even walked Brownie.

Everyone figured that the planes would be late. The time was uncertain. Which certainly meant there was plenty of time for that other piece of business. All he had to do was find a way to ditch Dessie.

Rules for Today and the Rest of Your Life

Dessie E. Gold, Paragon of Rectitude

☞ Wake up early.

☞ Wash your face.

☞ Brush your teeth.

☞ Brush your hair, one-hundred strokes.

☞ Stand up straight, shoulders back.

☞ Dress in a manner neither overly alluring or plain, positioning your hat to show your curls to your advantage.

☞ Apply a nice lipstick (red, but not too), making the most of your better-than-average-pretty-face-with-beautiful-eyes-although-somewhat-unfortunate-chin (according to Mother), bearing in mind that you are clearly in your prime (eighteen, to be exact) and your looks will soon fade.

☞ Refrain from overeating. Weight runs in the family. In fact, it wouldn't kill you to go a little hungry.

☞ Practice the piano. *Practice* the piano.

☞ Appreciate that *simply to have a piano* is a luxury during the Depression.

☞ Be grateful for that. (*We have sacrificed for you and your brother, in case you're unaware.*)

☞ The purpose of having the piano is to learn to play tunes that are delightful, that people like to hear, such as show tunes. Nothing depressing or heavy. (*Chopin, okay. Rachmaninoff, maybe. But for God's sake, Dessie, is there anything so wrong about Rogers and Hart, Jerome Kern and Oscar Hammerstein? Irving Berlin?*)

☞ Read the daily paper (the *Tribune*, not one of the rags, before your little brother cuts it up) in order to carry on a witty and informed conversation, as well as to express your heartfelt dismay where appropriate. The headlines are predictable, filled every day with feats of aviation (thrilling) and kidnappings (frightening) and Nazis (deeply disturbing), although reasonable people such as her father and, by extension, her mother feel confident that Hitler will not last.

☞ Walk and feed Brownie when Jay doesn't do it, which is often. (This isn't fair. Brownie is sweet but should not be your problem. You weren't the one who begged for a dog.)

☞ Polish your shoes. These are made of good leather, and *listen-to-me-missy*, they cost money.

☞ Eat with the proper utensils, in the proper order, gracefully, and never to excess, within proper reach. (Not to keep kosher—*enough is enough, this is America*—but certainly not to not eat pork and never ham, although bacon is permitted on occasion, as is shrimp, when dining in a restaurant, especially if dining with a boy whose example you might naturally follow.)

☞ With regard to the above, ask the boy plenty of questions and find the answers fascinating.

☞ Learn how to cook, although this can come later, after the engagement. (*But think about it, Dessie, how do you think food gets on the table?*).

☞ As for the boy, he will be someone like one of the cousins (though not, of course, one of the cousins and nothing like that imbecile Morris who calls himself Ace) but someone who will fit right in and not cause a disturbance. First choice, doctor or medical student; second, attorney; third, successful businessman. And after that—no, it's too soon to be desperate. And please, God, not too overly observant, not the kind who has to say a prayer over everything. The wedding will be held in the Windermere Hotel, which is perfectly lovely (everyone says so). Mother will see to the menu, the gown.

☞ Remember that you are Mother's one and only chance to give a beautiful wedding. (*Between you and Jay, your mother had still-borns, two girls lost, your invisible sisters. Never, never ask her.*)

☞ Don't upset Mother.

- ☞ See your own future. You and your groom and the appropriate in-laws your parents adore. Carrying lilies. Here comes the bride and here come the babies, the table full of dishes, the house full of guests, your name indelibly engraved on many future invitations to pleasant occasions, your fashionable clothing and ladylike laughter, the maid who comes to clean, the upright piano your husband has thoughtfully bought you, but what with the children and household and social commitments, who has time?
- ☞ Water the potted Jerusalem cherries, which are wilting in the living room (all the magazines say they're easy to grow, and still they keep dying).
- ☞ Stop it with the squinting. It causes fine lines.
- ☞ *Never* wear glasses.
- ☞ Always be meticulous, including with your penmanship.
- ☞ Drumroll—today! Take your little brother to the fairgrounds (again!) and stand in long lines for scientific, educational exhibits (again!) and even the infant incubators (once) but never the tawdry sideshows (it goes without saying) and eat Hebrew hot dogs dripping with yellow mustard (again, and it stains!) while waiting all day for the arrival of the seaplanes, which everyone knows will be late, and anyway, Papa says the pilot is a fascist, so he will not participate, but go ahead, take your little brother if you must, and Mother says, *Dessie, just be a darling.* But honestly, Mother overprotects him, worries over *criminal activity.* Jay is not a baby. He is already twelve. He can fend for himself. All it takes is a bribe, and a small one at that.
- ☞ Hide your secret diary under the mattress, in the center of the bed, where no one will find it. Place your other diary, the fake one, which Mother often reads, you can tell—she is a very bad snoop—in your top dresser drawer where she can find it again.

☞ Thank your lucky stars that nobody else heard the telephone ring, half a ring, in the hall, at exactly eleven o'clock last night when they were safely in bed.

☞ Give Brownie a hug. Whisper in his long, soft puppy ear. *Goodbye.*

What Would it Cost?

Dodo the Bird Girl, Formerly the Blind Girl From Mars, Formerly a Ward of the Great State of Georgia ("Wisdom, Justice, Moderation"), Formerly the Daughter of Someone, But Who Knows Who?

She feels herself fly in the first few moments of waking, the wind on her face, her thin limbs, her few tufts of hair, as if the sky can hold her, lift her, carry her and love her as nobody does.

She has never seen herself, her reflection. And why would she need to. People have said what she looks like, all her life. The world is light and form and shadow, a little bit of color, the warmth of the sun, the relief of the rain. The sweet and salty taste of food. Her face, she is told, is enough like a bird's that people will pay good money to look. She has never seen a bird. She has learned how to dress, in a costume of feathers, how to strut and how to cluck so they will laugh and then clap and then come back again, and bring friends.

Still. She doesn't mind it too much. Not like the place where she came from, with no light of day and no one to talk to and no one to listen, just every day moaning (her own? she couldn't tell) and screaming down the hall and hunger from eating nothing but mush and some of it rancid, and her arms tied down and her body cut open so she'd never have a baby and the scars she could feel with her fingers that were jagged and stank with ooze. The man in the night who did what he wanted, crushing her limbs, spilling her blood, spitting out names she will not repeat, not even in her mind. All of them believed she was incapable of speech, because she never spoke in there. She wanted to die.

And then she was summoned.

Taken.

His voice was smooth. He had observed her, he said, and he had chosen her. She was worth money.

He taught her what to do. First as the Blind Girl from Mars and when that didn't sell, the bird. *You understand me, don't you?* he said. *I bet you can talk if you want to, can't you. Call me Mr. R.*

There are others like her, plucked from asylums or rented from parents, but no one, he tells her, is just like her, and that is good, it is beautiful. *Freaks*, says Mr. R, *are the royalty of sideshows*. Rarer, of greater value than people who do things, swallow a flame, toot a horn with their ear. *You are special just for being you.*

They travel as a family, eat at a table. Mr. R. makes arrangements and pays them, cash, which she hides, with nowhere to spend it, no idea how. Here is what she likes: Mr. R never touches her. He sees she eats decent, even with just the two teeth she has left and both of them loose. Soups. Sweet cream. There is a soft place in him. Often, he leaves a little something outside for the ones who come hungry. He calls her Louise, a name she remembers, not Dodo, not stupid, not an animal or bird, except when she's working.

Louise.

And now, in this town of Chicago, this summer, there is a man, he is new, he is double her size, who opens his mouth and plunges a sword down his throat to his gullet and doesn't choke or cut himself. Nick. Nick Blades. He talks to her sometimes, touches her tiny arm but doesn't hurt her, steadies her. Words stick in her mouth from years of disuse. They slur without teeth. They coat her tongue. He is willing to wait. He brings her Coca Cola, fizzy and sweet, and some kind of candy, a heavenly cloud, that sticks to her fingers and melts in her mouth.

He bids her good night. He says that—*I bid you goodnight*—which nobody else has ever done.

Most places are the same, but this one is special, more than just a carnival. It's jam packed crowded, day and night. There is always something extra to bring people in—a parade, a swarm of music, the sounds of the horns floating over to them, the echo of drums, sometimes a *major extravaganza*. Hundreds of people on a stage outdoors and more than a hundred thousand in the audience, Mr. R said, they were Jews and the show was their story, *Romance of a People*, and such a big draw that they ran it again. She has never seen a show except the one she performs in. As for a Jew, she doesn't know what that is.

Here is a rule: Freaks can't be in public, wherever you please. This makes sense. Who will pay money if people can see them out in the open? Plus, they are working, not here to play. But Nick and the flame man can take off their costumes and walk right out however you wish, like anyone else. Miracles, he tells her, machines you never dreamed of. They even have tiny babies in ovens and the heat doesn't hurt them, not one bit. Imagine that.

No one has griped a lick until now, but something has changed. There is something that is coming. Melinda, who once let her touch the lush hair on her chin, says it's called an armada, twenty-four seaplanes, from all the way over the ocean, once in a lifetime. *Please, could they just this once have the afternoon off? And anyway, who will buy a ticket to a sideshow when everyone alive will be out at the lakefront?* The Midget City mayor has already announced they will close after lunch.

Why can't you just look up? is what Mr. R answers. *Stay where you are. It will be in the sky, for heaven's sake.* And he laughs a little laugh.

For a minute they agree. Then Eddie the half-wolf clears his throat. *Couldn't we just this once be like everyone else? What would it cost?*

And then it's on everyone's lips, those words. *What would it cost?*

Your Name in Print

Jack Morton, Obituary Writer (But Not for All Eternity)

Everyone he writes about is already dead and not even famous. He never gets celebrities. His job is to sum up the life of the average stiff from the city of Cicero (almost Chicago—so, so close, a hop and a wish). A few column inches.

> Respected/beloved community member.
>
> Factory foreman/salesman/nurse/owned a nice shoe store or restaurant/half-decent artist you never would have heard of.
>
> He enjoyed ball games at Wrigley Field.
>
> She liked to bake pie.
>
> This or that committee.
>
> Church.
>
> Devoted mother/father/aunt/uncle (never happens)/bachelor (wink if you know what that means).
>
> "Long illness" (cancer, keep it quiet). "Short illness" (flu or something flukey but just as often alcohol or drugs). "Accident" (suicide, maybe, occasionally auto, or sometimes the poor fellow fell off a ladder.) Heart.
>
> Survived by ... TK.
>
> Etc.
>
> -33-

Every reporter with a pen and an elbow to shove his way in will cover the airborne armada today, in print and on the radio. The star of the *Trib*, Philip Kinsley, is no doubt licking the tip of his pencil, assured of a front page byline, again. Whereas he, Jack Morton of the *Cicero Times*, all but sold his mortal soul for a press pass and entry to the Century of Progress on his Saturday off, and by gum, he will pound every sticky inch of pavement, peer in every corner, till he finds himself a story, a gem, a tip to call in to the *Trib*, one singular thing to make the editors acknowledge the fact of his existence, for once in his frustrated, wrongly anonymous life, so help him God.

The World Is Full of Pockets

[Name Redacted], Private, Specialist

Today is a record, an unsurpassed feat, and it's not even noon. The time in Chicago is 11:58 and twenty-six seconds. Twenty-seven. Twenty-eight, according to a fine gold timepiece known for its precision, a classic in design, which will never grow old, which he acquired in the course of a previous endeavor. It is even engraved. *Rufus C. Dawes.* The fair's president. There are no coincidences, not in this life. Only tricky situations, in this case, involving the maid and a type of complication he would rather avoid, whereas this, this fair—this is cotton candy. This Century of Progress, this summer of abundance is a godsend if ever there was one. And mother of God, he is good at what he does. The barely perceptible jostle, the gentlemanly touch of the elbow, gallant, as if steadying a lady as she enters the Café de Alex, with its tablecloths and orchestra, the white-gloved sanctum for those who wish to dine among their kind whilst gracing the fair with their pedigreed presence, apart from the gristle and grease. The liberation is a miracle of elegance and grace. By the time she registers what is missing from her European purse, he is gone, a soul she never saw.

Out among the masses, awe is swell for business. The marching bands. The pageants. *The Romance of a People,* the story of the Jews, brought a fortune for him. And every day, the Great Hall of Science, revealing the very essence of life, the art exhibition with portraits by Whistler—transcendent! The Hall of Religion, with every conceivable path to salvation. The struggle of humanity to understand unanswerable questions, the reasons things happen, the meaning of events . . . Jesus. Zeus. And on the wall, the Promised Land, Moses included. A whole Mayan Temple erected for show. This is reverence for profit, so why not his? Did he not earn it? Did he not darken the earth with his blood and his spit in the trenches? Did he not witness his only little brother blown open to the bowels? It was the war to end wars, and how long will that last? Give it a minute till the whole bloody world is at it again, as best he can tell from that two-cent *Trib*. His mother mad with grief. His father dead of the Depression. Money. He will take what he can get.

Hundreds of fools struck dumber than dumb each night in the dizzy Streets of Paris and the view is not bad. By day, they gape at premature babies and midgets and freaks. His act is unseen. He has the nimblest of fingers, the sharpest of eyes, a God-given talent. Imagine if she, oh faithless one, could see him now. Few of his marks, it is safe to conjecture, report their misfortune. This is a silent, private rebuke. Nobody likes to admit to being stupid, and anyway, what's to be done? Tell a cop you were robbed but didn't notice who did it? And of course he looks respectable, refined, not one of those godforsaken bastards who hide in the shadows, living on other people's trash. He can hide in plain sight.

Look at these dupes. The traveling salesmen, the housewives dragging their children through the cultural exhibits. The out-of-town lovers serenely believing they will never get caught. A couple of dollars, perhaps a missing necklace, is the least of their worries. It's just an inconvenience, a valuable lesson. A service he performs, if you will.

All day long, the crowds are kept informed with loudspeaker announcements, this and that way to dispense with their money, a "free" demonstration, the lost-and-found youngster to please retrieve from Traveler's Aid. And now, ladies and gentlemen, General Balbo's arrival is—yes!—delayed, possibly later than late afternoon, the time is uncertain.

Not for him. The time is 12:04 and forty-six seconds. A donut is in order. Powdered sugar. And coffee. The crowds are growing thicker. And here is a boy who has just this very minute given the slip to his pretty older sister, who doesn't seem bothered. Binoculars. Expensive. Money in the pocket, you can bet. But no, there are standards, morals he upholds. Children are off-limits.

The Song Is You

Tobias "Toby" Weber, Jr., Pianist, Salesman (Temperamentally Unsuited)

The time he had given her, the time they had agreed upon, was one p.m. Did she misunderstand? Did he? He was early by almost a full half hour. Dozens, hundreds of people pass by, and none of them her. Strut, walk, saunter. Shuffle, limp, slouch. A torturous game he plays with himself: how many synonyms for walking? This one is practically skipping over here. Amble and stroll. Step, step, step. His heart is swiftly beating to a metronome of misery. A world of wrong answers: Young, old, decrepit. The drab and flabby middle. Hats. Shoes. Skin of every color from blue-black to pallor. A smattering of words, not all of them English. German he can understand, Italian he can't, or maybe he can, a little. *Ammazza!* Syllables whose origins he can only guess. Polish? Hungarian? General Balbo is late in every language. And more to the point, so is she.

Constellations of girls, fat dandies swaggering past their prime, a trio of sausage-eating ladies who could have been his aunts and thank God they aren't, he'd have to add lying to his list of sins. But where oh where is she? One-sixteen, according to the gentleman he has just asked. Why did he tell her the Homes of Tomorrow? There are twelve different homes. Is she lost? She frequently squints, he suspects she needs glasses; perhaps she can't see him? Maybe he ought to move from this spot. But then what if she's here and he's there?

Last night it made sense, it sounded romantic: The Homes of Tomorrow. No one he knows will run into him here, at least he doesn't think so. Does he? His sisters have already viewed this exhibit and chattered about it, prefabricated walls you can just stick together, *one, two, three,* a snap of a finger, and full of machines like the one that washes dishes, a miracle if ever there was one, if only they were rich, which they aren't, but a person can dream. His father will wait in his store all day, praying for the chime that means a customer has entered, has stepped past the threshold. Every day the radio is playing—The White Sox when possible, customer favorites (if only there were customers): Vallee and Armstrong, Crosby, Astaire, and all this summer—live from the Century of Progress!—every kind of pageant and wonder, explained to the folks who cannot go. His father avoids the news that is disturbing. Better not to speak of it. And anyway, it wouldn't please his customers (if only he had some). Already, it doesn't help that he is German. People don't like them, not since the war. But everybody likes to hear a radio, and anything is better than the silence of that smothering emporium of furnishings that nobody wants. Dark and unbudgeable dining room tables, sedate upholstered chairs. A sofa to lie down and die on. The future is sleek, its components interchangeable, but no, he won't listen to his daughters or his wife, his piano-playing son. (*My son is my son, but disappointing,* Toby hears his father think.) And furthermore who will go shopping today? Today of all days? Half of the city—the half with any money—will be out at the lakefront. But even one sale is better than none, his father had said, while releasing his daughters from their weekly obligations (rearrange the toss pillows, slap out the dust, empty the ash trays, run a damp cloth, greet every person who walks through the door—assuming anyone does—as if they were family). So then it was clearly a matter of justice—*Geh, wenn du must, go if you must*—and anyway, it wasn't as if, in his months of apprenticeship, he, Tobias Jr., putative heir, had sold much of anything. A couple of lamps choked in hideous fringe, a telephone stand for your granny. Dreary. Lugubrious. The home of the past. Speaking of which, his mother will spend all day in her kitchen, with her head in a cloud of aroma and heat. Strudel, sticky with molten apple sugar. Buttery nutmeats. A kingdom complete with its own weather system, impermeable, so that he, Toby, is safe from his mother's appraisal.

Elsie, Anna, Greta—all three of his sisters are here at the fair, without any notion (he hopes!) of what he is up to. He pictures them flirting at the Black Forest Village, or watching that gal making ice cream from junket, or clapping for grain shot straight out of guns to make cereal for breakfast, not the sludgy porridge they were raised on. Automated magic. There is even a robot that can smoke a cigarette. Even better, in his sisters' opinion, are the miniature babies in ovens, if they have enough quarters to see them again (and here he feels shame about what he has done). Greta, the youngest, lives for the paintings in the art exhibition, and she will point out that seeing them is free with the general admission, and maybe the others will indulge her, or not. Elsie will long for the Venetian glass that catches the light in every color, next door to the Italian Pavilion, which is going to be packed, impassable. Not one of his sisters cares about the airborne armada, as best he can tell, but history is happening, and later they can say they had seen it. Twenty-four seaplanes arriving in formation. Really, unless you are a pilot or Italian, how much does this matter? It doesn't, to him.

His passion is music, flights of angels. A language any ear can understand, can receive at any time. Rachmaninoff. Tchaikovsky, Liszt, Brahms, Chopin. Beethoven. Wagner. A universe floating on a note, a world conjured with your fingers, even on the shabby old piano his mother had inherited, that poor wretched instrument of wood and warped fibers, the tusks of hunted elephants, the keys with which to enter the divine.

His passion is Dessie. Where is she?

A Pleasant Exchange

"Why, of course. I have one-thirty-one. And twenty-seven seconds. Twenty-eight, to be exact. Are you waiting for someone?"

Here It Comes

Thomas Finnerty, Jr., Chicago Police Department

Here it comes. The trouble he knew was inevitable, one way or another.
Three cups of coffee. An off-tasting hot dog. Everyone's nerves are on
edge and no one has slept. His toe has not healed, big toe on the left,
from tripping off a curb, he hates to admit, nothing heroic, just clumsy
and it's broken and too bad for him. He is stationed in the Gladiola Garden, across from the Italian Pavilion. Breathe. The chief made it clear—
every living, breathing cop, every body who can walk, is on duty-today,
all over this fair, like ants on a log (but inconspicuously), plus private security. Everybody's eyes must be everywhere at once, including the eyes
in the back of their heads. Mayor Kelly has spoken. Son of a cop (same
as Finnerty) and only in office a couple of months, since the previous
mayor, Cermak, was assassinated, shot point blank while standing next
to Roosevelt himself. Fortunately, not on their turf—it was in Florida. No
one can blame the Chicago P.D. But awful just the same. Then the temporary mayor, and now Mayor Kelly, and now what's important is the
city look good, not a hellhole of crime, not a slaughterhouse of livestock
and people.

Rufus C. Dawes, the fair's President, has made his wishes known.
Not a single mistake. Not a hair off a head. But also, *do not scare the public*. Keep
it under wraps. The whole place is lousy with radio yappers, reporters
from here and all over. The *Tribune* is one thing. They are okay. We have
friends over there. But there are dozens of others, rags. Plus *Time* magazine. And the new one, *Newsweek*. And also, the airwaves, coast to coast.
NBC. CBS. And also—the whole force knows it, but let us repeat—the President is paying attention, and over in Italy, so is Mussolini. And Hitler,
you'd better believe it.

So—to repeat, again! Nothing can happen. But—common sense, pri-
oritization. A kid skips a gate, let it go. A case of sticky fingers, miss-

ing wallet—sorry, Mister. There isn't time for booking petty crimes. The things you need to see are the knives and the guns smuggled in past security. You need to see the blade before it sees the light of day. You need to be quicker than a bullet. You need to have both eyes wide for bad actors, the glint in the eye of a kidnap, real or fake. There's a plague of them now. Two weeks wasted just this month, looking for a con-man who staged his own abduction. If they can prove it. But—listen up. Nothing. *Nothing.* <u>*Nothing*</u> will be worse than if a bomb goes off, even a small one. There have been threats. Credible ones. Do not say a word. Not to your wife, not your mother, not your girlfriend, not even your priest.

Here is what Finnerty would need to confess, if he dared: He is scared all the time. He would rather be anything else, a teacher, a baker, possibly a crook if he's honest about it, at least he'd get rich, but his father was a cop and his brothers are cops and so he is a cop and that's that.

His stomach is turning from that questionable hot dog. Why did he eat that? His headache is fierce. His toe throbs. And here is a wretch who is stealing the gladiolas right out of the garden, sneakily plucking. Probably intending to sell them. Do nothing.

Do something. Quick. Before you puke in plain sight.

Tempus Fugit

Rufus Cutler Dawes, President, The Century of Progress, Civic Leader, Visionary

Each and every time he looks at his wrist, he is displeased to see it's bare. He has questioned the maid, who has been of no use. As for his wife, he would rather she be none the wiser; the watch was a gift, she is bound to be upset. There will be tears, recrimination. It is apt to turn up. It can't have simply disappeared. It isn't magic.

Meanwhile, the time is 2:38, according to the waiter at the Café de Alex, where, for the first time today he has a minute to himself (until someone interrupts him). Better to avoid the Officer's Club, which is private, but not for him; he'll be accosted nonstop (was this one or that one perhaps inadvertently left off the list for this evening's events? As if it were he who has seen to these details.) At least he has a chance here, if only a small one, of not being bothered. The orchestra is playing Oscar Hammerstein, "The Song is You." The lunch crowd has thinned.

Time is truly flying. And so, thank heaven, is General Balbo. The takeoff from Montreal was clean, if hours late, just before noon. Here on the ground, every last preparation is in order, every detail meticulously planned and observed from every angle in advance. The viewing stand for dignitaries, honorary speeches, the provisions for the press, the dinner at the Drake (and why don't they pester Reed Landis; it's he who's in charge), and three more days packed full of receptions, including the photo with the Indian Chief in full, feathered headdress. The weather is perfect, hardly a cloud. He conferred with both Landis and Kelly an hour ago. There are men in black shirts and black ties who have gathered at the lakefront, but so far no sign of disturbance.

Still, there is uncertainty. According to intelligence, the fleet won't arrive until close on to six, but no need to share that with everyone yet. The vendors are happy. The longer it takes, the better for business and this is important, if the Century of Progress is to realize a profit. Money and genius are coiled together, intertwined. The great Hall of Science! The whole of Fort Dearborn! The city's reputation. So—to the people who said the Committee was crazy, staging this fair in the depths of the Depression—just look around. Millions of visitors, a blessing for Chicago, for the whole of the country. But nothing has been on a scale like today.

He should order something light. Not steak, which will cause indigestion again. He ought to save his appetite for tonight's gala, Helen would tell him. She is getting ready, her hair is being done, whatever women do. He ought to reduce. But who can predict, for certain, what tonight will bring about? In fact, he deserves this. He earned it. *Steak au poivre.* Chicago beef, the French preparation. And potatoes *au gratin.* And a glass of red wine. Because you never know what the future will bring.

Un·cer·tain

/ˌənˈsərtn/

1. not able to be relied on; not known or definite.

"an uncertain future"

Synonyms for *uncertain*

capricious
changeable
changeful
fickle
flickery
fluctuating
fluid
inconsistent
inconstant
mercurial
mutable
skittish
temperamental

Intelligent Precautions

Melinda the Bearded Lady, Last Name None of Your Business

The one thing that saves her, the one thing that stands between her and her furious beauty, is the hair on her chin. She will never shave it off. If she did that, how would she live? As somebody's wife? A rich man's mistress? Dependent on sex, on youth? No thank you to that. And while she is at it, she would rather see you laugh than have your pity.

Go ahead, snicker. Men are such fools. Nick with the swords is sweet on Louise, little Dodo. An improbable love if ever there was one, but who is she to judge? Who even knows what that girl understands. She hardly speaks. And if she did, God knows what she would say, what she has seen with her near-blind eyes.

Cluck, cluck.

Nick has snuck out between shows with Blaze the flame man, in search of a hat from the souvenir hawkers fabricating memories, emotional moments—something must cover the birdgirl's head, her scalp, which is almost as barren as Melinda's chin is ripe. A hat will obscure the girl's beakier features. An intelligent precaution, she has to concede.

Because Eddie (a sheep in wolf's clothing if ever there was one) is right this once. They are all of them going to the lakefront today, they are all of them going to witness the arrival, no matter the cost.

Will Mr. R. fire them? No. He is dependent on them. The truth of it is, he is nothing without them.

Her part is easy. She will go as a man.

And Who Is He Now?

Tobias (Toby) Weber, Jr.

Yes, she had to first bring her brother to the fair, which got her out of Hyde Park, with unaccounted hours when her parents wouldn't wonder, or his, for that matter, since Balbo, as everyone knows, will be late (the loudspeaker confirmed it), and the crowds provide cover. But why not go straight to Union Station, just as soon as she had Jay taken care of? He should have said that. He wished he had. Why hadn't he? Is she somewhere nearby? Did he somehow not see her? Maybe she is right around the corner! But how could that be? What is she wearing? The blue dress with flowers? Maybe she has gotten delayed with her brother. Maybe she is lost (but that doesn't seem like her). Maybe she is standing at another entrance. Hours, an eternity has passed. Maybe, oh God, did she change her mind? Last night she sounded definite. Didn't she?

There is one more thing he can do, should he do it?

His whole life savings is stuffed in his wallet. The little bit his father had paid him (it would never be enough, who was he kidding), and—this drenches his heart with remorse—some of the bills that his father kept hidden under the cushions, distrusting the banks, plus some from his sisters, and, yes, his mother, her sturdy, heavy satchel, awful, he knows, but they will have to do without it, it can't be helped. In time they will forgive him, they have to, and he will pay them back, they will see, yes, they will, he will redeem himself completely. How this will happen, exactly, he doesn't quite know, but he has faith. He will make it all right, and they will come to love Dessie.

Love.

Adore.

Revere.

She had entered his life through his ears, before he ever saw her. It was May of '32. Still chilly in Wisconsin, the lake still cold, but July was too expensive for vacation, even a short one. The homey resort where they went every year. The owners were German—Christian, of course, he'd thought everyone was, at least that he'd met—but families came from Milwaukee and Sheboygan and Chicago, even, apparently, Jews, if they weren't too religious. How could he know? In the middle of the day, the little stage for the evening's entertainment was vacant. But it wasn't. There was music. There was Dessie. *Moonlight Sonata*. Her smile, a secret smile for herself. There was someone who loved what he loved as much as he did, who felt what he felt, and she was young and she was pretty, and her eyes, which were limpid and green, held every kind of expression. Her fingers on the keys were full of grace where his were clumsy, untaught. She was everything he'd wanted in his cramped and lonely life. She lived in Chicago, and so did he. She was south and he was north. Her parents would forbid this. So would his. His sisters would not be the least sympathetic, not even Greta. And so they met in secret, for more than a year now. A signal on the telephone. A letter from a make-believe address. Twice this summer they had visited the fair (although she had seen the Romance of a People with her parents, her brother, her cousins, of course not him). The university near her address, with its wide green lawns soaked in sunshine. The library in winter, redolent of books, of piped heat. The Loop, under elevated trains that rattled on the tracks overhead. Just once in Thalia Hall, the cheapest seats. Still. There was time enough for Dessie to decide, to be sure about him, as he is sure about her. She is eighteen, of age, and he is nineteen, and there will never be anyone else for him.

Their love is impossible, and yet they are living in a world where everything is possible. Just look around you.

Another Pleasant Exchange (Everything Is Possible)

A fire-eater and a sword swallower go for a walk. The sun is high in the sky. They come upon a robot that can smoke a cigarette.

"Will you look at that thing?" the fire-eater says.

"What's the big deal?" the sword swallower says.

"Well, what if those robots replace us?" the fire-eater says.

"Robots will never replace us. Know why?" the sword swallower says.

"Why?"

"Who cares if a robot can swallow a sword? You need humans to do the things that humans can't do."

The fire-eater huffs. And with that they turn back, because their act is up soon.

Something Must Be Done

Madame Amalie Louise Recht of France, Head Baby Nurse, Infant In-cubator Exhibition

Here they come again. Day and night, there are boys, as well as cheap grown men, who pay the quarter admission to look at the babies, smug in their belief that they alone know the trick. You can walk out the back and jump over the gate, straight into the strip show they call the Streets of Paris.

Something must be done. The Streets of Paris? Ha! Nothing is Parisian about that place, except that lust knows no boundaries. A bosom and a pair of long legs has no language.

No one is French around here except her, and this includes her boss, who has a generous heart but is loose with the facts—his nationality, credentials. German is unfortunate and so is being Jewish. She knows he is scared. He has taken to saying that his training was in Paris, whereas hers really was. Sometimes she misses it. Home. Her scattered brothers. Her lovely mother tongue. But this is her calling, this life on the midway. Americans would let these babies die. They are "weaklings" in a country where being strong is everything. All over the country, preemies are dying, doomed despite decades of knowing how to save them. Machines and skilled nurses. A standard of hygiene. Breast milk. Love. How hard could it be? How much would it cost? But over in the great Hall of Science, they are teaching eugenics. Why save the weak? The only thing to do is appeal to the public, put on a show. Propaganda for preemies, her boss likes to call it. Her role is *Madame*. People will pay to look at babies on display. She will slip a diamond ring up a preemie's skinny arm and say something in French. *Voila!*—with the price of admission, they have paid for the child to be saved. *Merci.*

Nights, she will sit up for hours, hearing the music and applause, the drunken yowls from the booming Streets of Paris, over the thin little cries of her charges with their unformed lungs, their tiny hearts.

That girl, Sally Rand, the fan dancer, is entirely American, although rather sweet. She came through once, to coo at the newborns, days before getting arrested the first time. A nice enough girl, just down on her luck. She was Lady Godiva at the start of the season. Americans believe she is indecent and they can't get enough.

Today, the incubator exhibition is especially crowded. Her boss is at the gate, shaking hands, his wife is bathing babies. Soon the crowds will leave for the lakefront. Everyone is waiting for word of the impending arrival of General Balbo, the airborne armada, the great display of power. She has better things to do. She has a very sick baby to tend to, under two pounds and looking dangerously blue and cyanotic.

These boys are underage. One has fancy seeing-glasses hanging from his neck. She can sense he wants to linger. There's a spark in his eye when he looks at the babies. Maybe he will learn something new. Maybe his generation, these children who've never seen war in their homeland, who've suffered the Depression but have never been reduced to eating rats to survive, as her parents had done, during the Siege, maybe these children will be better, kinder. One can only hope, although the news is not good. The other boy is older and impatient. She doesn't like the look of him. His friend calls him Ace. She doesn't like the way people cheat—really steal—to see that girl prance around, dressed up to look naked, until the police come and yank her offstage. *Something must be done.* But not by her. She is not the boys' mother. She doesn't have time. And anyway, Ace and Ace's protégé will soon enough discover that the Fan Dancer doesn't perform until evening. And then, mark her words, they will shrug their boyish shoulders and head to the freak shows.

The God's Honest Truth

Madame de Fortuna, Crystal Ball, Fortunes Read, Psychic, 10¢

If she could, she would give back the dime. She would tell him to have all the fun he can have. She would hug him if she could. But she can't. She is professional. This is her job.

She says, *The sky is the limit*, and now he is happy.

The Only Story Today

Pietro DiSanti, Greeter-at-the Gate, Italian Pavilion

Third time today that reporter, if that's what he is, is sniffing around here. Itching to get to the bottom of something, any kind of story, call in a tip, get his name in the paper. For God's sake! Can he not see, can he not get it through his extremely thick skull that Pietro is busy? Jack, that's his name, *Name's-Jack, how-de-do,* and what a pest. *See anything colorful? Any human interest?*

Pietro knows more than a few choice words, and he would use them now, if he weren't at the gate in a professional capacity, the very soul of courtesy, in English and Italian, the mile-wide smile.

There is only one story today, and that story is flying high in the sky. That story is the pride of all of Italy and everybody here in this pavilion. Already last night, Pietro was up until four in the morning, the neighborhood covered in red, white, and green, blood singing in their veins, their voices ringing in the air. Tonight, please God, when the fleet arrives safe, they will never go to bed, maybe never again.

He ought to be tired, but he isn't. For once in his life, his feet don't hurt from this stand-up job, and for all he had to drink, his head does not ache.

Thousands of people are already down by the water. His parents are there. They've been waiting for hours, since early this morning, to get the best spots (aside from the seats for the VIPs), to maybe, *lodare Dio!,* catch a glimpse of "his" face, to see the 96 men upon arrival. And hundreds of people are here in this pavilion, milling, killing time, with their souvenir hats, their pictures of Balbo and Il Duce, waiting. Some of them are wearing black shirts and ties. The armada is late, the time is three-sixteen (as long as they're safe!). But suspense is making everybody nervy and upset.

The last two announcements were only for someone to fetch a lost child (and why don't these parents pay better attention?).

But one thing is certain. General Balbo will not let them down.

The restrooms are that way. Welcome to Italy!

Jack-the-reporter is scribbling notes. He could strangle that guy. There's a cop by the gate, another cop across the way in the Gladiola Garden, he can see him from here. Tip of the hat.

Venetian glass? That way. These girls are so pretty. The one with the squint looks almost like Anna, except for her chin, which is not a sweet heart. Anna has promised to visit, with or without her two sisters. At least he can see her, if only for a minute. *Watch your step.*

Theft

Elsie, Anna, and Greta Weber, Sisters

"Look, is that Toby?" Greta says.

"Why would he be over there?" Anna says.

Greta doesn't know.

"Do you really think our brother would be visiting the Homes of To-morrow? Toby?" Elsie says. "That's the last place he'd go!" She is angry, and also hungry, because somehow, money is missing from the pocket-book she carries, a dollar, which could pay for a lot. Her sisters are missing money too. Did someone pick their pockets? But how could that be?

"Should we look?" Greta says. "Just to see?" She really and truly thinks it is her brother in the crowd in the distance, looking forlorn. Toby is sometimes a readable book. He thinks she doesn't know about the girl that he sneaks out to see, the one from last summer. Seriously, he underestimates her. She will not say a word. But something isn't right.

"Don't we see Toby enough?" Elsie says. "Besides, that isn't him. And we still have enough to split another hot dog."

Maybe she is wrong. Which pains her. How, Greta thinks, can she not be sure that her brother is her brother?

Balbo is late, it is almost 4:00, and their stomachs are rumbling.

Anna has her by the arm. She wants them to go to the Italian pavil-ion, she's been nudging for hours. "Are you coming?" she says.

An Unpleasant Exchange (No One Can Know)

Finnerty! Hurry! But quiet. Quick! (But my God, he looks sick, what's the matter with him?)

"But—"

No buts. Do not start a panic. Backup is coming.

"But—"

Quick! Hundreds of people are in that pavilion—

"But—"

Move!

What Is the Matter?

Morris "Ace" Katz, Future Pilot, U.S. Army Air Corps

"Will you look at this one? Cluck, cluck. Here, little birdie, can you fly? Oh, come on, Jay, relax. You said you wanted to do this."

Sometimes his cousin is fun but sometimes, like now, he's soft, like a girl. These are freaks. Mistakes of nature. What's the problem? Still, he would have killed to see the Fan Dancer dance. Even if she wasn't entirely naked, like some people said. The plan was pure genius—sneak in the back and no one would ever notice their age, plus they wouldn't have to pay (except for the quarter to see the freak babies). It was Jay after all who'd figured that out. Terrific idea. Too bad it won't work. It figures she doesn't go on until late. And no, they can't stay past Balbo's arrival, it's moving on 5:00. Already, his cousin is in trouble with Dessie, Little Miss Perfect.

Cluck, cluck, cluck. May as well make the best of it. "Come on, Jay. The fire-eater's next."

An Announcement

4:57 p.m.: *Ladies and gentlemen, General Italo Balbo and his airborne armada are expected to arrive within the hour . . .*

What He Saw

Pietro DiSanti, Greeter-at-the Gate

No, he didn't get a good look at her face. He is sweating through his shirt. He thinks he might vomit, feels it rising in his throat, a riotous rush. The cops have the box that the woman delivered, thrust into his hands and then simply vanished, like magic, he thinks, although he knows better. The box is addressed to General Balbo. No, it's not ticking, at least they don't think so, but it's highly suspicious and goddamn, that goddamned reporter, that Jack, goddamn him to hell, he could wring the guy's neck, he's all over this thing, and thank God, everyone is leaving the pavilion, they are all but stampeding to the water on the heels of the announcement. If only he could go! But he can't. The cops keep asking all the same questions, again and again, and the answer is no, he doesn't know (and he could strangle himself).

The truth of it is this: To his utter disgrace, he accepted the box without looking at her, because he thought he saw Anna out there on the walkway. Of course he can't say that. The truth he can say: In that single split second, he figured the woman was delivering a cake, which he has to admit makes no sense whatsoever.

Stam·pede

/stam'pēd/

noun

1. a sudden panicked rush of a number of horses, cattle, or other animals
2. a mass movement of people at a common impulse

Synonyms for *stampede*

Charge
Panic
Dash
Chase
Rush
Route
Flight

Even A Cold Heart Beats

You May Call Him Anthony

Today has been the luckiest day of his thirty-six and three-quarters years on earth, beyond his fondest conjuring. His fashionable satchel is utterly stuffed and so is his belly. For the first time ever, he went in the Café de Alex, and ordered a steak and, for the first time since his wife left him, ate every bite, every morsel, as well as the potatoes au gratin, and the spinach with cream, and all of the bread, which came with real butter, and drank a little wine and listened to the music, and stained the cloth napkin with savory blood.

Life is abundant. And yes, he is blessed. He survived a near miss, a close brush, by the skin of his chin. For one heart-crushing instant, in front of Fort Dearborn, his number was up. Done. Perhaps it was justice, punishment for living when his brother had not, for being stupid with his wife, for contriving the theft of a watch from a pillar of the city, a trophy, as if it would bring back time he has squandered, for being the same age (almost!) as General Balbo, with nothing but damage to show for himself. Surely, that cop saw his hand in that purse. He would rot in some jail. It would serve him right. And then, to his utter amazement, the cop simply shrugged and walked off.

It is almost a sign. But of what?

There are times in this life when a man must act.

He will witness the airborne armada, high in the sky, with everyone else, and give Balbo his due. He will keep his hot hands to himself for once.

And one thing more. That fellow, that desolate bastard waiting the whole afternoon at the Homes of Tomorrow (jilted, stood up by a woman, it is written on every fiber of his body)—if he sees that poor soul on the way to the water, then he, who is, after all, named for a certain saint, is going to do the one thing he has never imagined. You know who you are, what you are capable of doing. And yet, in the end, nothing is certain.

Missing Person

5:06 p.m.: *Attention, Miss Dessie Gold, please meet your party at Traveler's Aid.*

Flight

General Italo Balbo, Commander of the Fleet, Lead Plane (SM 55X), First Squadron (Black Star), 1-BALB

It's crowded up here. Six men in his plane, "1-BALB": co-pilot, mechanic, radio man, guest engineer, plus the Italian ambassador who came aboard in Montreal (to translate, and also, perhaps, to look over his shoulder). Black stars on the rudders. Twenty-three craft, eight squadrons, each in a vee, are following them, and over them, the U.S. Army escort of 42 planes. The noise of the engines enters their bones, rattles their breath. The radio is squawking, aural dots and dashes that connect them to earth.

He has seen things that few will see, captured his impressions, arranged them in words: *"geometrical patterns of water and meadowland, brimming canals meandering like ribbons of crystal amidst tilled fields and tiny gardens, factories enclosed with hurdles and wooden fences and equipped with quaint balconies and verandas, which make them appear like toys ... Tiny steamboats are puffing busily hither and thither. In front of our eyes, towns with black and white ... appear and vanish."*

And he has seen things that he will not write. Fifteen days and sleepless nights. The very air conscious, alive with perception. The spectrum of sky. Ninety-five fellows betting their lives on metal shells, mechanical propellers (one is tractive, the other propulsive; pull and push, inhale and exhale). Betting their lives on him. He lost a man. Ugo. Ugo Quintavalle. Drowned outside of Amsterdam, and four others hurt, a plane broken apart. And yet there is nothing to do but fly.

Fly on.

Through wind and through ice with its fierce, seductive danger, its cold wink of death. Cigarette smoke choking the cockpit, fog out the windshield. Wing and a prayer. The voice of Benito Mussolini forever in his head and on the telephone line more than once upon landing.

The cold is unbearable this high up, exquisitely painful. Yet he is sweating. Cognac helps. A sip, another sip. Another breath. Each day wondering if this is your last. Same as war. Same as life. Are you ready?

Here it comes. Five years of planning, of mapping, of training (relentless), of unquestioning devotion. Il Duce is his leader, his light, who gave him command of the Air Force, who lifted him here, to the cusp of this historical feat. This is not about speed. The American pilot, Wiley Post, flying in the opposite direction, is faster. He, Italo Balbo, is spectacular. Sublime in formation.

At times, his mind travels to his wife and his children (and also his mistress). But every thought today must be for Italy. Fascism triumphs! The fleet has prevailed. In just a few minutes, he will see the crowd waving, cheering at the shore, where they will all—all 24 planes, all 96 men (and, yes, the ambassador)—alight in the lake, the blessed water.

And yet.

Something has happened. Il Duce is proud, he is delighted, but at each successive landing, as the crowds grow thicker and confetti rains down (despite a smattering of Communist detractors), something is there, like a shadow. Like he is a shadow. Like he is obscuring the Source. He must always reflect the Glory of Il Duce and yet he has become the center of attention.

It is a dangerous place.

He belongs to his country. Yet nowhere is home. He no longer belongs to the earth or to the sky or to the water. He belongs to this moment, which is already ending.

To land enfolds everything, beauty and achievement, relief, exhilaration, loss. Sensations for which there are no words in any language.

Soon there will be marching bands and medals and wine, and finesmelling ladies, and telegrams from every word leader. His face in every paper, his voice on all the airwaves.

Chicago. He can almost see it. He can almost hear the cheers. And he already knows: For as long as he lives, there will never be another flight like this.

Dominion

Burton LaSalle, Mayor, Midget City

When he looks at the sky, as he does every morning as the sun comes up, he is only as small as everyone else.

Midget City is closed. He has shut the place down for the afternoon and for all of tonight, for them to gather by the water, husbands and wives, neighbors and friends, rivals in affection, wounded and loved, citizens all, of the city they've created by willing its existence, as with any city.

People can stare at them. Suit yourself.

From around the great earth, from beyond the horizon, the seaplanes are coming. They are calling it "The Roaring Armada of Goodwill" in all the papers, on the radio.

He wishes for them, the people who live in his city, to see what he sees, to feel what he feels: Boundless.

Ahem! Piece of Cake

Jack Morton, Reporter

Five tough cops. The whole east wing of the Pavilion cleared, the gate-keeper dismissed (and off to the water he went, clutching his Miraculous medal). Yet he, Jack Morton, was permitted to remain. Or, to be honest, overlooked in the commotion, but the only thing that matters is to be in the room. Listen, this story is worth risking his life.

"Stand back from the box."

"I need to puke."

"Shhh!"

"Careful!"

Breathe.

"I am opening it."

"What the—"

"Oh, for God's sake. Did you ever?"

"What?"

"It's . . ."

"What?"

"Cake."

"Cake??"

"That is what I said."

"It's a cake in a cake box."

"Please."

"Vanilla."

"*Please!*"

"I think it's butter cream."

"See for yourself."

"What's it say?"

"Finnerty, go find a can, for Christ's sake."

"Give me your knife."

"Are we going to—"

"What?"

"You have a better idea?"

"Hey!"

"Why not."

"You!"

"Shame to let it go to waste."

"Hey! You! Who the hell let you in here? Out! Before I arrest you!"

Nickel in a payphone outside the pavilion, next to the Gladiola Garden. The number is busy, but never mind. He has typed up the item in his head:

```
A square package, suspected of containing a bomb, was
delivered to the Italian Pavilion, addressed to Gen.
Italo Balbo ... Inside the police found a small cake
and ate it.
```

The *Trib* will of course seek verification. Answers to questions. Yes, it was vanilla, and yes, there was icing, red, white, and green, and yes, there was a message, smeared and misspelled: *Congradulations.*

Congratulations

Rufus C. Dawes, President, The Century of Progress

He is seated at the head of the VIP section, next to Mayor Kelly and Governor Horner, and Helen, and the wives. Everything has happened exactly as planned. In advance of the arrival, the Sky Ride has halted, the children's Enchanted Island has closed, and most of the exhibits must surely be empty, as hundreds of thousands have taken their places, all along the shore.

It is almost six o'clock, by his guess, but no, he won't question the time, not with Helen by his side. A thrill is in the air, a collective vibration, all but palpable. A beautiful day, with not a single incident, according to the latest report from the police chief. Minutes from now, God willing, he will meet the arrivals, shaking each hand, and later share a toast at the glittering gala. To Balbo! To friendship! To mankind's achievements! If only they will use them for good.

In the blink of an eye, he has become an old man. He is a product of a world that no longer exists, its cities and its countryside powered by horses, its nights lit by candles, by gaslamp, by moon and by stars. In two weeks time he will turn sixty-six. This—this Century of Progress, this will be his legacy, long after no one remembers his name. Thousands of young men and women, children, are here on this shore. He has written in invisible ink on the future he will not live to see.

The Radio Is On

In a furniture store in Lincoln Park, there is not a single customer. The store closed at 5, without a sale today. And yet the owner remains, sitting by the radio. The broadcast is live from the Century of Progress. Later he will walk back home to his wife's sweet kitchen, his daughters, his son who thinks he can't understand what it means to love something you cannot have. Later. In time. For now he is listening. For now he is envisioning the city he came from. Dresden. The Jewel Box of Europe. For now, in his mind, he is walking its streets, he is seeing its castle, its sky.

In a Hyde Park apartment, a man and a woman listen to the radio, a small brown dog at their feet. National Broadcast Company. *Live from the Century of Progress!* The man and the woman and their daughter and son have visited, of course, most recently on Jewish Day, to see "The Romance of a People," the crowd-pleasing pageant. The timing of the show was no coincidence, the man knows well. The national Zionist convention was meeting at the Palmer House hotel. Eight million dollars, in addition to the ticket sales, were pledged for German Jews. The plan is to resettle them in Palestine—as many, as fast as they can.

Today is the Sabbath. The sun will not set for another two hours, but the man and the woman are not so observant as to disallow the radio. This is a modern American family. No, he will not celebrate this General Balbo, this fascist armada arriving in "friendship," and yet he cannot deny his son, who lives for aviation, the spectacle of flight. He cannot, to his surprise, deny his own curiosity, his grudging admiration. There is really no reason, he says to his wife, to suppose that this Balbo is anti-Semitic. She is half-listening, here but not here. She is thinking, as she so often does, of her children, living and dead, tiny sparks that went out. The man who will one day die in her arms is thinking of the future, and he is afraid.

A Prayer Is Answered

Madame Amalie Louise Recht, Infant Incubator Exhibition

They have left her behind, the visitors, the nurses she has trained, her German boss and his American wife. They have locked both the gates, front and back. Someone must stay. She is holding a baby no bigger than a whisper, who, in spite of all odds, is pinking up.

Do Something Worth Doing

Tobias Weber, Jr. (Toby)

He has been here for hours, patiently (or maybe impatiently) waiting at the Homes of Tomorrow, refusing to know what he knows to be true. It is too much to bear. He has been robbed, his heart ripped from his chest. She isn't coming, not now and not ever. His life is now over. His future is gone. And so is his wallet, a fact he encountered in the late afternoon, when he finally thought to have something to eat. His money and identity. Stolen. And what does it matter? Who is he now? There is nothing for him. He has nowhere to go, not a penny to his name. He can never again show his face to his father, his mother, his sisters, knowing what he knows, what he has done. He is worse than a fool, he is a man without purpose.

Now what?

He is surely condemned to slip off in the shadows, live among the people who slither through the alleyways, eating people's scraps. He will die a sad death. Alone.

Someone has done what he dares not do, what he thought about doing all afternoon and dismissed as inconceivable, the height of indiscretion. *Miss Dessie Gold, please meet your party at Traveler's Aid.* Someone has spoken her name, for all the world, to smite his heart. Should he go there and see? But no, he's been rejected. And what did he expect? Why would she marry a wretch like him? Why would she leave her whole family behind? What made him believe? Yet earlier today, he felt her presence. She was near him, he could swear it.

Impossible. The world is not magic. No one is psychic.

North and South cannot meet.

And he cannot stand in the same place forever.

Who cares where he goes? He is swept in the river of flesh when it happens. Him. That man. One of the many who had given him the time, many hours ago when his soul was intact. The man is tapping his shoulder, thrusting a fistful of money in his hands, a thick wad of bills, as if he is mad, as if the whole crazy world has slipped off its axis. "Forget about her," the man says. "Take my advice and do something worth doing." And how can this stranger know about Dessie? Can a person read a mind?

Can a body simply vanish? Evaporate? Into thick air.

Toby is clutching money in his hand, who knows how much. *Do something worth doing.* Look at this wad! However much it is, it is multiplying fast in his head. A fortune! Behold! He can go far away, he can travel the world, see all the great cities, mountains, seas. All of heaven and earth are his for the taking! Or . . . he can go back home.

The Rest of Her Life, in Three Parts

Dessie E. Gold

She had stood there and looked, from a few feet off, in her blue dress with flowers, her hat at an angle, her lips soft red. She didn't need to squint to see what was before her:

Toby is waiting, exactly as he said he would. She loves him, she does, or she thinks that she does, although she doesn't feel a spark. Should she? She loves that he loves her, loves who she is in his eyes and no one else's. People are everywhere around her, but no one might love her like this again, the way he does. She isn't really beautiful. She isn't someone special. She isn't even gifted at playing the piano, she knows this. She scarcely has friends. Her own little brother has ditched her, before she had the chance. She is sure he's gone off to find Morris. Ace. There is no one at all on this earth for her. Except for Toby who adores her, Toby who is waiting. And yet she can't move, can't utter a word.

Sometimes she pictures her two lost sisters walking beside her, pretty young girls, a pair of confidants—to talk to, to teach, to discover one another. She has no one like that in real life. She has only her diaries—the real one, the fake one, the one she is continuously writing in her head, and the one that is lying in repose beneath the words. She keeps making up versions of Dessie, composing variations of a woman, and none of them is right.

If she leaves here with Toby, who will she be? Can she hurt her own mother? Her mother must love her, even if she never really listens, even if she reads a phony diary and never really sees the only daughter who is living. How can she devastate her father, who doesn't look well, who is pale, who worries all the time? She would even miss Jay, the little brat. Even Brownie.

But Toby.

No matter what she does, she will break someone's heart, never mind her own. It is all her fault.

She stands and time passes. She turns and she enters the Homes of Tomorrow, looks at every model, uncomprehending. Mechanical and sleek. Prefabrication. Homes composed of pieces, interchangeable with anybody else's, and no kind of refuge.

There he is, still, when she comes back out. He is looking at the ground, and she takes a step closer. *Go.* Claim your future. But where will they go? To Union Station. To elope. After which, they have no plans, they have no money. No home. Toby is a dreamer.

What time is it now? She is slipping away, feeling sick, infected, as if by her existence she's contaminating everything. She walks and she walks, only vaguely aware of the Pavilions she is passing.

Hey, Missy, smile.

Why the long face?

Welcome to Italy.

Miss, can I buy you a Coke?

Rules for living today: Do not respond. Do not look back. Do not ruin his life, along with your own. Because their love will not last. Because the woman he loves is a vision, a creation. Because he loves magic that comes from a piano. Because he wants with all his heart to be able to do what he believes she can do, as if by love he can inhabit her. He loves what he believes she can give him, and she can't.

Dessie—her name in her head, the way she speaks to herself. Dessie, do this. Dessie, do that.

And then it is coming from outside her head. *Attention, Miss Dessie Gold.*

Who is summoning her? Should she go? Is it Toby? Would he be this bold? Did he wait this long? Did he not give up? She will go after all. If he loves her this much. She will leave it to fate.

❈ ❈ ❈

It's Jay. And Ace. They are impatiently waiting at Traveler's Aid, and they appear to be at odds. Jay has their father's expensive binoculars. How did she fail to notice this morning? (Well, of course, she wasn't paying attention, now was she?). Her little brother actually hugs her, for once, and for once she doesn't flinch, despite the grease on his shirt, which will get on her dress and not come out.

She says, "I won't even ask."

And they are walking to the water.

And Ace says, "Yes, and where were *you*?"

❈ ❈ ❈

And now: Here they are, among hundreds of thousands of unknown people lining the shore, a single living organism, each soul distinct and indistinguishable.

History is happening.

She feels it in the air.

Time is uncertain but there isn't much left: Before the airborne armada fills up the sky. Before the cheers ring out. Before a ring is on her finger the very next summer, and then a month later, she calls the wedding off. Before the world is at war. Before her father is dead ("long illness," according to the obit). Before the boys enlist. Before Ace flies 52 missions with flawless precision, before coming home to his elegant wife. Before Jay dies in the sky, in flames over Nuremberg, trying to free a crewmate who's trapped. Before she buries her mother. Brownie. Before she grows thin as a knife. Before she writes stories, books about make-believe people, which are popular successes. Before she is a woman wearing glasses. Before she finds love late in life in a way that she never imagined, with somebody like her and further off-limits. Before she finds peace.

For as long as she breathes, she will return to this day. Toby, of course, who she will never see again. More than anything else, she will inhabit, over and over, this crystalline moment near the water with her cousin and her brother, the awe of the crowd, the breadth of the sky, the sheer joy in Jay's voice as he stands there besides her, lifting their father's binoculars higher, and cries: They're here!

Not a Feather on Her Body

Dodo, in Disguise

The hat has wings. They're made of felt.

Nick has a steadying hand on her back. Melinda is wearing some-body's trousers, standing beside her. Eddie. Blaze. They are waiting by the water like everyone else, when a cry rings out and words swell and echo up and down the viewing stands and all along the shore.

"Look!" says the flame man. "Look, do you see?"

She doesn't, not yet. She feels her feet on the ground. She feels the air on her face. She feels something she will never be able to contain, a self that connects to the pulse of the earth. She can see it in her body when the sky begins to roar.

General Italo Balbo, 1896–1940
Cause of death: friendly fire.

The Fire-Eater

The intimacy is what she craves: her head tipped back, her open throat, the torch. The tongue of an incendiary lover. Night after night, the world arrives anew.

She is claimed by the spectacle of fire as a child, by a vision of a sideshow performer, from long, long ago. She is tiny in the flesh, enormous in shadow. Salt and dirt and sweat. And here is a man-shaped god, who bares his chest and singes the air with great plumes of flame, reeking of creation and destruction. It is her destiny revealed.

The trick, she knows now, is in the exhale.

Combustion, applause. Flesh against flesh. Light of her life.

The euphoria she feels in the moment of extinguishment: the world and its cities and its bodies disappear. She is released from the limits of time.

Historical Notes

Boundless as the Sky is a work of fiction, but Balbo's historic flight to the Century of Progress World's Fair was real. As reported by the *Tribune's* star reporter Philip Kinsley, the fleet made a perfect landing at 6 p.m. Chicago time. Under the headline "Notes of the Italian Flyers," a tiny, unsigned item read: A square package, suspected of containing a bomb, was delivered to the Italian Pavilion, addressed to Gen. Italo Balbo . . . Inside the police found a small cake and ate it.

Time magazine reported that "a youth with binoculars" was first to sight the seaplanes.

All of the exhibitions cited were real, and some characters are based on historical figures.

Italo Balbo helped bring Benito Mussolini to power in 1922, having become a fascist organizer after WWI. The arrival of the "roaring armada of goodwill" was met with thunderous applause and three days of receptions in Chicago, followed by a meeting at the White House with President Roosevelt, a tickertape parade in Manhattan, and congratulatory telegrams from world leaders from the Pope to Hitler—all of which reportedly caused Mussolini to be jealous of his own airman. Balbo's fortunes turned sharply when he argued against an alliance with Nazi Germany, the only member of Mussolini's inner circle to do so. By the end of 1933, he was sidelined as Governor-General of Italian Libya; he died in an incident of friendly fire on June 28, 1940. The description of what he saw from the air is in his own (translated) words.

Wiley Post completed the first solo round-the-world flight just a week after Balbo's landing, on July 22, 1933. Post died in a crash on August 5, 1935, along with the humorist Will Rogers.

Rufus C. Dawes was the president of the Century of Progress and one of the visionaries behind Chicago's Museum of Science and Industry, which opened the same year. I have no reason to believe that his watch was stolen or that he ate at the Café de Alex that day. He died on January 8, 1940.

Madame Amalie Louise Recht was the head nurse at the infant incubator exhibition on the midway. The exhibit was next door to the burlesque hall where the fan dancer, Sally Rand, performed. Although the infant incubator exhibition was very popular in its own right, people discovered they could pay a quarter admission, exit through the back, and jump the gate into the Streets of Paris, a situation that was corrected when the fair opened the following summer. Along with her boss Dr. Martin Couney and his wife Maye, Madame Recht ("Aunt Louise" to those she knew) helped save the lives of some 7000 American babies over a 40-year run at various world's fairs and amusement parks. She died on April 15, 1951.

Dodo the Bird Girl is based on Koo-Koo the Bird Girl, whose real name was Minnie Woolsey and who was "discovered" in an asylum in Georgia. Minnie is believed to have had Virchow-Seckel Syndrome, which accounted for her tiny stature, birdlike face, near baldness, and near-blindness. She can be seen in the 1932 movie "Freaks." Although a popular performer during the 1930s, there is no evidence that Koo-Koo was at the Century of Progress; however, she did have imitators. Koo-Koo took up residence on Coney Island around 1936 and died after being hit by a car in 1960. Australian performance artist and disability activist Sarah Houbolt currently performs an homage to Koo-Koo on stages throughout the world. I was fortunate to see her at Coney Island/Sideshows by the Sea.

Jay Gold is a salute to the "Raffel boys," who visited the Century of Progress and went on to serve in the U.S. Army Air Corps during WWII: Mark Raffel, Fred Raffel, and in particular Sgt. William P. Raffel (1925-1945), B-17G 43-38596—837th Bomb Squadron, whose aircraft was shot down over Nuremberg. His surviving crewmates reported that he died trying to save his trapped crewmate before the plane exploded.

To this day, there is a Balbo Drive in Chicago, and a Roman pillar gifted to the city by Benito Mussolini in 1934, commemorating the aviator's flight.

Additional Historical Notes

The Fan Dancer: Sally Rand (1904-1979). Desperate for money during the Depression, Rand talked her way into a burlesque show in The Streets of Paris, which made her famous. She continued to perform burlesque for the rest of her life. At the time of her death, she was broke.

The Double: Betty Lou Williams (1932-1955). Believed to be an "incomplete" conjoined twin, she spent her life as a midway attraction. An x-ray purportedly showed a second head inside her chest. Williams' earnings paid for all of her siblings to go to college. She died at 22.

The Balloonist: Bela Probstner (nineteenth century, exact dates unknown). Probstner's brother-in-law, Pál Szinyei Merse, immortalized him in the painting "The Balloon," which can be found in the Hungarian National Museum in Budapest.

The Lover: Milena Jesenská, Franz Kafka's lover and Ravensbrück prisoner number 4714. She was sentenced for writing articles criticizing Hitler and for smuggling Jews and political refugees out of Czechoslovakia.

Where Graves Have No Names: Kisvárda, Hungary, where some of the author's relatives are presumably interred beneath a soccer field.

Acknowledgments

For their careful reading and invaluable suggestions, I would like to thank Kim Chinquee, Terese Svoboda, Charles Salzberg, Angela Himsel, Christina Chiu, Elise Zealand, and Helen Zelon. Thank you to Chip Brown and "the Salon," Tara Lynn Masih, John Madera, Anca Cristofivici, Pamela Ryder, Janice Eidus, and Jill Caryl Weiner for friendship and inspiration. Thank you to Cherie Raffel, Joyce Raffel, Maureen Evers, and Richard Beach. Gratitude to Melanie Jackson, for being in my corner. And thank you to Mikhail Iossell and Summer Literary Seminars for inviting me to teach in many cities, including "the city where dogs lie dreaming."

For the research behind the story of Italo Balbo's historic flight, I am indebted to the New York Public Library, where I had the good fortune of being a scholar in residence—with special thanks to Melanie Locay and Eleanor Yadin. Information about the Century of Progress exhibitions, from the Midget City to the cigarette-smoking robot, came from the University of Chicago Special Collections, the Daley Library at the University of Illinois in Chicago, and the Chicago Historical Museum. I am endlessly grateful to the archivists who preserve what they can of our vanishing history.

Huge thanks to Jacob Smullyan for giving these words a home.

Above all, thank you to my husband, Mike Evers, to our sons Brendan and Sean, and to my office assistant, Pierre the terrier, who slept through most of it.

Dawn Raffel is the author of five previous books, most recently *The Strange Case of Dr. Couney: How a Mysterious European Showman Saved Thousands of American Babies*. Other books include two short story collections, a novel, and a memoir. Her stories have appeared in many magazines and anthologies, including *NOON, BOMB, Conjunctions, Exquisite Pandemic, New American Writing, The Anchor Book of New American Short Stories, Best Small Fictions*, and more.

ALSO BY DAWN RAFFEL

In the Year of Long Division (1995)
Carrying the Body (2002)
Further Adventures in the Restless Universe (2010)
The Secret Life of Objects (2012)
The Strange Case of Dr. Couney (2018)

CPSIA information can be obtained
at www.ICGtesting.com
Printed in the USA
LVHW041310281222
736019LV00003B/57